P9-DWZ-337

Owen B. Greenwald

Up the Stakes
The Big Bet: Book #2

Written by Owen B. Greenwald

Published by EPIC Press™
PO Box 398166
Minneapolis, MN 55439

Printed in the United States of America.

Cover design by Candice Keimig
Images for cover art obtained from iStockPhoto.com
Edited by Ryan Hume

LIBRARY OF CONGRESS CATALOGING-IN-PUBLICATION DATA

Greenwald, Owen B.
Up the stakes / Owen B. Greenwald.
p. cm. — (The big bet ; #2)
Summary: Living large after the successful heist, Jason is approached by a mysterious patron with a very risky job for him: rig a basketball game in Las Vegas. The job itself doesn't interest Jason so much as the reason the boss wants Jason for the job—the entire situation looks like a test. Needless to say, Jason plans on passing.
ISBN 978-1-68076-184-9 (hardcover)
1. Swindlers and swindling—Fiction. 2. Deception—Fiction.
3. Young adult fiction. I. Title.
[Fic]—dc23

2015949054

EPICPRESS.COM

For my family,
particularly Mom and Dad,
without whose love, support, and understanding
I would not have come this far

ONE

THEY SAY CRIME DOESN'T PAY. WELL, LEMME TELL you, they're either stupid or lying. The criminal lifestyle's very rewarding, if you're talented. And I'm the best there is.

My most recent payout? Three million dollars. Of course, it was split four ways with my partners in crime, but that's still not bad, for a profession that "doesn't pay". But then, you already know all that. I don't need to tell you how my last job went—or how in the aftermath, my team deserted me. *Disbanded*, if you'd prefer I be polite.

I can already hear the exemplars of virtue lining up to point out that the loss of my team—my friends—just goes to show that crime doesn't pay. Again, they're wrong. It's more like this: Crime pays . . . but it'll cost you.

Anyway, this is why I was actually paying attention in Statistics. For one thing, I wasn't engaging in any long-term plotting (protip—during class is a great time to plot). Back when the Club for Perfect Cleanliness still met, I'd spend Stats running back the day's business. Now, though, I had nothing major to think about. I was still running Van Buren's monthly blackjack game, but the legwork for *that* was several years finished, and profits were shrinking. It wasn't doing anything at this point but keeping my mind sharp. Brains are use-it-or-lose-it—and I didn't intend to lose it.

For another thing, as long as I was focused on the lesson, I had an excuse to not look at Kira.

Kira's one of the coolest people I know, and she's saved my ass more times than I can count. She, Z, and I founded the CPC as a front for all sorts of disreputable activities, and we'd gotten pretty close over the years. She'd promised me right after the split we'd stay friends.

So much for that.

Just two weeks later, and even *she* wasn't speaking to me anymore. The last straw'd been just a few days ago, when she'd blown up after I'd suggested she was missing the CPC's shenanigans. I mean, she *totally* is. Kira's an adrenaline junkie, and a normal high school lifestyle just doesn't give her the stimulation she needs. We could all tell she was going crazy without an outlet, but apparently, I wasn't allowed to say it.

In my mind's eye, I could still picture her, eyes and mouth sharp as razors, radiating pure fury like an avenging angel. *If you try to pull me back in one more time, I swear I'll rip off your dick and shove it up your asshole!*

Kira isn't the most eloquent, but she has a refreshingly unique way with words sometimes.

I could almost *feel* her simmering behind me. High school's a draining, miserable, soul-sucking experience at the best of times, but for Kira, it's a special kind of hell. She wanted to be anywhere but stuck behind a desk, listening to a teacher drone on about sample size. And not so long ago, I'd have turned around and given her a sympathetic look, let her know she wasn't alone. But now I couldn't, and Kira didn't have anyone else who could.

Thinking about Kira made me think about Addie, which I'd been trying my best not to do. It was hard though, especially during history, when she couldn't just blend into a crowd to avoid me (as I suspected she did between classes). Everything about her reminded me what a great team we'd made—right down to her dark hair, close-cropped in the name of the job.

She'd meant more to me than just an asset, too. But I couldn't keep dwelling on the past when the future had no shortage of pressing issues.

Lucas, for instance.

I *had* to let him know I'd done something major, but I could hardly just *tell* him I'd ripped off a bunch of poker players. For one thing, it was illegal, and while he *probably* wouldn't report me to the police, he totally *might* just to teach me a lesson. For another, it'd be a bitch to work into casual conversation, amplified by the fact that Lucas and I don't really *do* casual conversation.

So instead, I'd dismissed my driver and hired a new one myself (No, I don't have my license yet—being a criminal mastermind takes a lot of time. And if you thought *Lucas Jorgensen* was gonna take time out of his schedule to drive his son to school, you don't know Lucas Jorgensen).

It was a complete waste of money, but I had a six-figure profit from a single job. I could've hired people to sit in the car and talk with me on the way to school, and my bank account would've barely noticed. Besides, it wasn't about the money, it was about sending a message. A message that, admittedly, Lucas hadn't acknowledged, but it was only a matter of time before he broached the subject. Right now, he was trying to figure me out without the shame of asking for a hint. How long would it take the old bastard to admit I was smarter than him? How fucking *long*—

I glanced down at my notebook and noticed the pencil's point had snapped. Sighing, I reached for my pencil sharpener. As long as thinking about Lucas still provoked that kind of reaction, I couldn't pretend he was a nonissue in my life. A good psychiatrist could've probably cured me, but beating Lucas at his own games would too. And *that* would be much more fun than twice-weekly talking sessions.

The bell rang just as I was tucking away my sharpener. I quickly copied down the homework, shoved everything into my bag, and left before Kira could get in front of me. I'd survived another day of senior year.

I pulled out my new phone—my *real* one, that is. Ever since Richard had gotten my last one, I'd taken to carrying two, so that if someone demanded my phone, and wasn't too careful about searching me, I wouldn't lose anything but a cheap blue flip-top with no redeeming features.

One text. Mason was waiting in the parking lot. I picked up my pace—no need to waste his time, after all. I was almost out the main door when—

"Jason Jorgensen?"

The voice was low and mild, yet authoritative. I stopped in my tracks and turned around.

He hadn't registered as I'd passed, a tall, broad-shouldered teacher I didn't recognize. At least, my first assumption was that he was a teacher. He was a little too well-muscled for a life in academia, but he wore the same business-casual ensemble as the rest—white shirt, gray slacks, pale green tie.

But donning business-casual attire was easy no matter *who* you were, if you wanted to look like a teacher. It'd be harder to reduce your muscle mass. And while I've known some athletic teachers, something about his stance set off my alarms.

"Who wants to know?"

The man glanced around the foyer, looking

pointedly at the number of people passing through. Then he closed the distance between us.

"Someone with a personal interest in New York's poker scene," he said, so softly that nobody else could hear over the chatter.

My blood froze.

"Let's walk," said the obviously-not-a-teacher, putting a massive hand on my shoulder. He began to steer me expertly through the crowd. I let him maneuver me, wondering if I should shout or something. He knew about the poker game—he could very well want me dead.

Then again, if *I* were trying to kill someone, I probably wouldn't do it at their school, especially during the busiest time of the day. There were thousands of better times and places. So it was maybe—*probably*—safe to play along. For now.

Nevertheless, I reached into my pocket and curled my fingers around my phone. Slowly, cautiously, I eased it out and waited. Sure enough, we soon came across a particularly thick knot of sophomores, and while my escort was navigating through them, I aimed carefully and snapped a couple pictures. I shot from my waist, so my aim was probably off, but hopefully I'd gotten *something* useful. I tucked the phone away again before he noticed anything.

We stopped in a small courtyard, a decent distance from the parking lot. I could see people flowing out of the main building, so I was still in shouting distance. That was reassuring.

Deep breath.

"Jason Jorgensen," said the man again, and this time it wasn't a question.

I braced myself. This was happening whether I liked it or not. "Let us, for the moment, presume I am that person. What do you want with me?"

"*If* you were that person, you'd have set up Roxy's poker game and walked out with a million dollars. Sound familiar?"

I forced myself to breathe normally, but my heart was pumping at a mile a minute. This was a worst-case scenario. I'd gone too far, pissed off the wrong people. And now they'd found me.

"Let us again—without confirming I *am* this person—assume you're correct. What of it?" I replied, throat dry.

"If you *were* Jason Jorgensen, and you *had* rigged the game . . . well, you'd have done something my boss called 'mighty impressive'. There'd be a job waiting for you, if you wanted it."

That was . . . unexpected.

"A job," I repeated. "Tell me more. I'm listening."

"You'll understand if I can't give details to anyone other than Jason Jorgensen himself."

He obviously knew he had the right guy. But he was offering me a chance to deny it, to back out without consequence. That, though . . . that, I couldn't do. Someone important had noticed my work. They'd thought it was *impressive.*

Of *course* I was gonna see where my ingenuity'd led me.

"I am indeed that figure-shrouded myth, that legend, that blackheart extraordinaire, Jason Jorgensen." I looked the man in the eye with my best cocky grin. "At the risk of repeating myself, what kind of job?"

"It's a simple thing. In two weeks, the University of Maryland will play against Duke University in Las Vegas for the NCAA basketball tournament. We'd like you to ensure the University of Maryland wins."

"You couldn't get anyone closer?"

"If you look at your calendar, you'll find that the week leading up to the game is your spring break. And naturally, your airfare will be paid. Distance won't be an issue."

"Alright," I said, noting to myself that he had avoided the question. "Give me a second. I want to think this over."

After thirty seconds of furious thinking, at least *one* thing seemed obvious—I was being tested. The job itself was unimportant, nothing but a milk run. A chance for me to prove myself to . . . someone.

Maybe I didn't want what this mysterious *someone* was offering, but I'd never find out if I walked away now.

"Okay. Who's your boss?"

Silence.

"Right, that's not something I need to know." I tried to sound professional. The man nodded curtly. "What about *your* name, then?"

His impassive stare didn't waver, so I decided to just pick a name and go with it.

"Then I'll call you Mr. Big for now."

"Fine with me," rumbled Mr. Big. "Whatever works for you."

I'd gone with his most obviously abnormal characteristic, but he wasn't *that* big. Kira probably could've taken him in a straight fight.

Kira.

That's when I remembered I was missing three-quarters of my old team. That seemed like relevant information to divulge, but I might not still have the job if my employer *knew* that, so I just asked, "What're my assets?"

"You will be provided a small budget," said Mr. Big. "And a small team of experts whose resources will be at your disposal. Anything outside of that is your responsibility."

Okay. That sounded pretty good. "So, just to make sure I've got it, you fly me out to Vegas for my spring break, introduce me to my team, we rig the game, I get paid, you fly me home?"

Mr. Big's short neck sank into his collar as he nodded once.

It sounded just as good the second time. But a decision like this warranted closer examination. "Mind giving me a few days? This is all so sudden, understand."

"Think all you like," said Mr. Big. "When you've decided, leave a rock on this bench. White for no. Black for yes."

I fixed the bench's position in my memory. And

then I realized what I should've asked all along. "What's my cut?"

I hadn't thought the question important, seeing as it wasn't impacting my decision in the slightest. But I should probably *pretend* to be motivated by greed, as that's probably how they were modeling me. The fact that I hadn't asked yet was probably setting off all kinds of red flags.

"Two hundred thousand. Fifty in advance, one-fifty after."

"Seems a little low, after my last job."

Mr. Big chuckled. It sounded like he was chewing gravel. "You're not robbing fucking Fort Knox. You do this job right, we'll see where things go. But it's not my job to talk you into it."

He turned to leave as if he considered the conversation over, but he hesitated, making sure I had nothing more to say. I didn't, so he walked away with slow, deliberate strides until he turned a corner and vanished from view.

The moment he was gone, I looked at the

pictures I'd taken of Mr. Big. Most of them were blurry messes, but one had come out clearly. The vantage point was terrible, but you could clearly make out his face.

Maybe it'd come in handy. At the very least, I could show my team and see if Mr. Big had recruited them too.

I texted Mason an apology and started back towards the parking lot, replaying the conversation to glean as much information out of it as possible. There was a lot, and I mean a *lot*, I didn't know about this job. That was bad.

But even so, I had no doubt I'd accept. This was an opportunity—you say yes to opportunities, because who knows when the next one will come along? Sure, I might run into problems later, but I could deal with problems. I was Jason Jorgensen, con artist, and I could deal with anything Las Vegas threw at me.

Besides, if I really wanted to outdo Lucas, I had to up the stakes.

TWO

MY BLOOD ITCHED ALL THE WAY HOME, AND knowing I couldn't scratch it for at least another week was *killing* me. Forget being attentive or productive for the foreseeable future—I was buzzing with plans, speculations, concerns. A "small budget and a team of experts"? Just what did that entail? It would've made sense to give me specifics as far in advance as possible, so either my mysterious patron didn't have that information yet . . . or they were interested in seeing what I could come up with in a limited time frame.

Whoever these people were, I was gonna show them just how impressive I could be.

In the meantime, there was plenty I *did* know, so I didn't have to just sit back for a week. For example, I could familiarize myself with the rules of basketball. If I could've only brought Z along, he'd have filled me in, no problem. I'd lost count of the number of CPC meetings he'd sidetracked bringing up a previous night's game. Becoming a sports expert had actually been on my short list for a couple years, just so I could formulate an intelligent response and revel in the shock on his face . . . but there'd always been more important matters. Ironic that I finally had an excuse *now*, after the CPC was already defunct.

The car halted outside my driveway and idled as the wrought iron gate slid slowly open. Lucas liked the gate because it was dramatic, but he didn't put much faith in it as a security tool—he saved his faith for the CCTV system, and the three teams of private security officers roaming the grounds and halls at all times. It wasn't a *huge* expanse—maybe one suburb-sized block—but for New York, it was practically Downton Abbey. The *wastefulness* of the place always ground my gears. It was impossible for two people to *use* it all, even with part of the house turned over to the security, the help, and the family butler. It was like the gate, house, and butler were more to stoke Lucas's ego than for any functional purpose. That's probably what I hate most about him, his towering ego. No wonder I'm so humble.

Jeeves coughed as I walked in, just loud enough to be audible. That was how he opened every conversation with me, that polite little cough.

"Welcome home, Master Jorgensen," he said in his impeccable English accent. "Can I get you anything to eat or drink?"

"I'm fine, Jeeves," I said, rolling my eyes like I did every time he asked. Jeeves was always waiting when I got home, despite the fact that I'd never taken him up on his offer. I'd finally realized he was monitoring the CCTVs for my car's approach, which means there'd been another hidden benefit of hiring Mason—for the first time ever, Jeeves had failed to recognize my approach. He seemed to have taken it as a personal insult, if his stiffness was anything to go by, but Jeeves would never let that color his professional interactions with me. He was the quintessential dutiful butler, and proud of it. I still wonder sometimes where Lucas found him, because I can't imagine him coming from anywhere but between the pages of *Pride and Prejudice*.

"Mr. Jorgensen is upstairs in his study," said Jeeves. "He asked not to be disturbed, but he wished me to inquire why Mr. Gorelic met with your disapproval."

I felt a small tingle of triumph. So Lucas *had* noticed. And while he was too proud to ask directly the questions he *really* cared about, he was prodding me with others, hoping I'd give something away. I'd been playing these games since I was four.

"He wasn't friendly enough." There, let Lucas read into *that*. "See you 'round, Jeeves."

I was halfway to the door when Jeeves coughed again, bringing me up short. "Mr. Jorgensen also wishes to know if he is expected to pay Mr. Mason's salary."

I turned around slowly to give myself time to write innocence all over my face. "Nah, I can handle it. Lucas didn't get where he is by spending money he didn't need to, after all."

Some bitterness must've crept into my tone, because Jeeves snorted with disapproval. "Your father—"

"—*Lucas*—"

"—would be more than willing to employ Mr. Mason if you are convinced of his suitability."

"He's been *not* employing Mason all his life, and it hasn't killed him yet."

Another snort. Jeeves was really good at communicating only using face-related bodily functions. He could probably do pretty well with the others too, but he was far too reserved for such vulgarities.

"One other thing," I said before I left. "I'm

spending my spring break in Vegas. I'm telling you now so you don't wonder where I am later. Lucas probably won't even notice I'm gone, so you probably don't have to tell him, but you can if you want to . . . and I know you want to."

Jeeves didn't so much as blink. "Las Vegas, Master Jorgensen?"

Like I said before, I'd made up my mind practically before the mysterious man had left, and even if I hadn't signed on *officially*, I had in my heart. There was no reason to keep the information hidden until it was "official", especially since I knew Lucas didn't care either way. That's the one benefit of being related to him—he doesn't care. In just about any other family (Kira's, for instance), there would've been a discussion, a quantifying of maturity, a safety lecture, and a possibility that I wouldn't be allowed to go. Guess I should count my blessings.

"Yep. Again, paying my own way."

"A wonderful choice, Las Vegas. Do you have

any plans?" Jeeves *sounded* curious enough, but I wasn't convinced he actually cared—one of his unofficial duties is to gather information about the other residents of the house. I knew—or at least suspected—that anything I said would be repeated back to Lucas later.

"I've never been," I said. "I'd like to see what the fuss is about. I'm keeping my schedule open, and we'll see where the week leads me."

This answer apparently satisfied Jeeves, who let me go without further protest. I scaled the two flights of stairs to my room in record time before he could call me back. Somehow, I could never find it in my heart to ignore him—he was so unflinchingly *professional* about annoying me that it was almost its own apology.

I tiptoed past the study on the way to my room, careful not to rouse the sleeping dragon within. Lucas was frequently engaged in work too important to be disturbed, but not so important that he couldn't get up and berate me for a few minutes every time he heard my footsteps. Blah, blah, blah, Jorgensen International, blah, blah, you'll have your own hedge fund someday, blah, not as successful as mine, of course—it was a common routine, one I usually escaped by pissing him off. This time, though, I was safe . . . although I made sure to shut the door quietly too, just in case. I eased my backpack off my shoulders and guided it to a soft landing on the pile of clean laundry Jeeves had left by the door, then flopped onto the bed and opened my laptop. Time to see what was new on Facebook.

Partway through my news feed, I scrolled past Addie's name and immediately felt hollow. It wasn't even a big deal—she was just sharing some stupid pun—but seeing the name put her in my head, reminded me how tense things were between us all. We could follow each other's lives on Facebook, but in meatspace, we barely talked to each other. If they'd just unfriended me, that would've made sense. It would've hurt, but I'd have understood.

This was infinitely more confusing. Was I allowed to comment on their posts? "Like" them?

And then there was the temptation to vaguebook about the situation and hope they saw it. I was resisting that temptation now, wrestling with the urge to post something like *big things ahead* and hope Addie asked about it so I could convince her to come to Vegas with me . . .

. . . No.

I slammed my computer shut. I didn't feel like browsing Facebook anymore. Instead, I started pulling outfits out from the pile of clothes. Might as well start the packing process now, since I'd decided I was going. That proved an effective distraction—for a bit.

I waited two days to leave the stone on the bench, figuring that it wouldn't be good to appear *too* eager. I didn't see Mr. Big again, but later that day, an email showed up in my inbox. The sender's address was a jumble of letters and numbers, but the subject was all too clear—*job*.

It was shortly followed by an alert from PayPal, telling me my account was fifty-thousand dollars richer.

Whatever part of me had been holding onto the possibility that this was some kind of joke vanished abruptly, and despite myself, I sat up a little straighter. This wasn't just taking money, this was being *paid*. This was *legitimacy*. I was a big-time, salaried criminal now, and things were only gonna go up from here.

The e-mail's contents were nowhere near as exciting, just a lot of boring—if necessary—information. Flight details, job parameters, et cetera. It also contained directions from the airport to the Mandalay Bay Hotel, where my room had been booked.

Your room is 843, the e-mail read. The door will be unlocked, and the key is inside. From there, you will make contact with the other members of your team.

I wasn't sure how to read that last bit. Would the others be waiting for me at the hotel? In that case, they'd already know each other, I'd be the outsider, and the power dynamic of the group would be weighed against me . . . and depending on their general attitude, that could be a problem. On the other hand, it could just mean they'd leave a list of phone numbers by the key, leaving me to call and assemble the team. *That* would give me implicit authority.

I needed more information—*real* information, not flight details and room numbers. Being kept in the dark was making me twitchy. Was *this* how the rest of the CPC had felt pretty much all the time? Now I understood why they'd hated it so much.

My first instinct was to have Kira dissect the e-mail, but asking her for favors was at the bottom of my to-do list right now. Besides, there's no way these guys hadn't covered their tracks. They weren't unsuspecting marks—they'd be prepared.

The next section of the e-mail confirmed my

suspicions that our employers weren't to be trifled with—a clear warning *not* to bet on Maryland ourselves. Any attempts, it warned, would be noticed and "dealt with". Call me crazy, but I wasn't too eager to discover what they meant by *that* particular turn of phrase. I could guess just fine.

It was a sensible rule—I'd have been suspicious if they *hadn't* touched on it—but I was still disappointed. Betting is fun; betting when you're sure of the outcome, even more so.

But even the money from a surefire bet paled in comparison to the job's *true* reward—the promise of moving on to better things if I impressed the people behind the curtain.

I just had to pass this test.

THREE

EVERY SURFACE INSIDE THE MANDALAY BAY HOTEL gleamed as if it'd been hand-polished by a particularly dedicated team of robots. The tiles gleamed, the chandeliers gleamed, even the walls gleamed. It was almost nice enough to make me forget I was in Las Vegas.

The plane ride had been so uneventful, I'd almost *wished* for a crying baby on board just to relieve the monotony. My neighbor had tried to make awkward conversation every five minutes no matter how uninterested I sounded. Even the in-flight movie'd been boring and uninspired. But the moment I'd stepped out of baggage claim onto the baking sidewalk and breathed a deep lungful of smog, I'd realized the airplane hadn't been so bad after all.

Spring break in Vegas. Woohoo.

The Mandalay Bay shuttle seemed to have calculated its route specifically to reinforce my first impression. Everywhere I looked there was grime. Sometimes, efforts had been made to disguise it beneath a veneer of opulence . . . other times, not so much. And yet, since planning the caper was pointless until I had a clearer picture of my teammates and their talents, I'd had little to do but stare out my dusty window and wonder why anyone chose to live here.

I don't mean to pick on it too much, though—I've seen worse. But us New Yorkers are competitive, and we like to trash other big cities. Makes us feel better about living in New York City, I expect. So to those of you from Las Vegas, I don't *actually* wanna raze your hometown to the ground and salt the earth (which I assume is what happened to the rest of Nevada). Just . . . try aiming for the trash cans sometimes.

Besides, as I said, one look at Mandalay Bay and I was ready to forgive everything. It radiated class—some might've called the decor tacky, but I have a taste for opulence. Even better, the scorching heat was swept away in a blast of conditioned air the moment I stepped through the doors. I was practically skipping and whistling show tunes as I rolled my luggage into the elevator, the interior of which was gleaming just as brightly as the rest of the hotel.

Now, with answers just eight floors away, my brain was itching. I was so *done* with maybes. I had until Saturday to draw up and implement a plan, and it was already Monday morning. If I wasn't so good at improvising, I'd even be *worried.* As it was, I was just annoyed.

But then, I suppose my shadowy evaluators wanted to see how I performed under pressure.

Fifth floor . . . sixth floor . . . seventh floor . . .

Eighth. The elevator doors parted smoothly and I stepped out into the hallway. From there, I simply followed the signs to my door.

I twisted the knob. It yielded.

I stood there for a few seconds, hand still wrapped around the knob. The moment I opened it, there was no going back. This wasn't some high school gang. This was the big leagues.

But in the end, of course I opened it. I'd been chasing the big leagues all my life, and no amount of reservations were gonna scare me off. I spent a few seconds running through my contingency plans—no sense in being unprepared—then stepped into the room, dragging my bag behind me.

"Who's there?"

It was a woman's voice, as polite as it was forceful. Entirely pleasant if it was room service, but just enough hostility to register to an intruder.

"Just a dedicated Terrapins fan here for the game," I replied. I shut the door, then dropped my suitcase by the wall. I couldn't see much of the room from here, but it looked nice and large. I deemed it an acceptable base of operations—provisionally, of course.

"Finally, someone else shows up," said the woman. Her voice reminded me of something, and I tried to place the memory as I walked down the hallway. The closer I got, the louder—and more familiar—her voice became. "I've been here since—"

I recognized Addie's voice the exact moment she came into view, and abruptly froze as my brain refused to believe the signals my senses were sending.

"Why are *you* here?" she demanded, hands balled on her hips.

I flailed about mentally for an explanation. Not my finest moment—you've probably already figured out what was going on—but I'd been caught off-guard by Addie not only being in Las Vegas rather than New York, but in *my* room.

"I, you—"

"Never mind," said Addie flatly. "It's obvious. I shouldn't have asked."

I shifted beneath her glare, putting the pieces together for myself. There was really only one reason for her to be here . . . and her attitude signaled loud and clear that she was blaming *me*. Which was actually a pretty reasonable conclusion, from her perspective . . .

"I promise I didn't set this up," I blurted out.

Her gaze became probing, and I didn't hesitate to meet her eyes. After a few long seconds, she turned away, apparently satisfied. "I believe you," she said. Either she was a lot calmer than she had been, or she'd decided to hide her anger—with Addie, it was almost impossible to tell the difference. "So we both got noticed."

"Yup."

"And now I have to work with you. After what you pulled last time."

I pulled a chair away from the coffee table and sat opposite her. "I've mentioned I'm sorry, right?"

"Only a few dozen times." Following my lead, Addie took a seat on the couch. "Apologies are cheap. But that's all personal crap, and we're on payroll. I can be professional if you can."

There was no warmth in that voice, but it was a step toward reconciliation. "I'll take an olive branch when I can get it," I said. "Deal. One hundred percent professional."

"And being professional includes *sharing things with the group*."

I sighed. "I *get it*. You don't need to keep bringing that up every few seconds."

"Well, since you apparently need *reminding*—" Addie took a deep breath. "Right. Professional."

She crossed her arms and gazed around what would be our home for the next week. "Bedrooms are through those doors," she said, in an attempt to change the subject. Her face, though, hadn't lost its coldness. "There are two, so I'd say four other teammates is a good upper bound, though it's probably fewer. You don't know, do you?"

"I'm in the dark, sorry." I shrugged helplessly. "Who got you? Big man, brown hair, round little nose . . . actually, one sec."

In just a few swipes, Mr. Big's picture was open on my phone. "Yeah, that's him," she said immediately. "Showed up after school one day—"

"—Me too. He must've gotten us the same day. Tuesday?"

"Same day. Do you know why he picked *us*?"

"No, but I've got a hypothesis. This is less about the job, and more about how we do it. I think it's a test—a trial run."

"I thought about that. You're saying someone noticed our last job, somehow discovered our identities, and thought we might make good recruits?"

"There's a lot of unknown in that explanation," I admitted. "But it's all I can come up with. Not like it changes anything though—we'd wanna do our best either way."

"Right. I suppose."

"And whatever's actually going on, it's good

talking to you again." I slipped that one past my tongue before my brain could veto it, and immediately regretted saying anything. Addie pursed her lips and looked at me like I was a stain on the carpet. A carpet she owned, that is, not *this* one. She didn't even deign to respond. We sat silently for what felt like hours, but was probably about a minute.

"Got any ideas yet?" Addie asked at last, again steering the conversation away from any awkwardness.

"I figured I'd wait until I knew the full extent of our resources," I said, relieved. "Our mystery employer hasn't exactly been forthcoming—my only guaranteed resource until a few minutes ago was me. Now it's me *and* you. I can't make the plan without knowing what I'm working with."

"I guess that makes sense."

"So I'm the second person to show? You really haven't seen anyone else?"

"Nope," said Addie. "Got here yesterday morning. My e-mail told me the room was taken care of and that I could just walk in. I settled in, called home to let *Mamá* know I was safe, and I've been waiting here since." She gestured at the window. "City's been taunting me since I arrived, but I didn't want to miss a teammate's arrival."

I shrugged. "Well, I hope the rest don't keep us waiting. We're on the clock."

The next person arrived several hours later, after Addie and I were already finished comparing our conversations with our recruiter, highlighting commonalities and differences. I'd moved on to unpacking and was in the bathroom designated as mine, finding a place for my toothbrush and toothpaste, when I heard our door open.

I was curious about our new arrival, but not so curious that I didn't stick my toothpaste behind the sink mirror before I made for the living room. I was halfway down the short hallway when I heard a loud, "No *fucking* way," and broke into a run. I recognized *that* voice right away.

"Wait!" That was Addie's voice. "Let me—"

I skidded around the corner, dreading what I

knew I'd see. Sure enough, Kira stood in the antechamber. Hearing my footsteps, she lifted her head and looked at me with a face like a thunderstorm. I met her eyes as calmly as I could, which felt a lot like maintaining eye contact with a hungry tiger.

"Of shitfucking *course*," she said venomously. "Mr. Big Shot himself."

"It wasn't him!" said Addie.

"Bull*shit* it wasn't him."

Kira advanced towards me, eyes flashing with the promise of violence.

"C'mon, Kira . . . " The words should've come out calm and controlled, but my voice decided to do its own thing and squeak. Any hopes that Kira hadn't noticed were dashed when satisfaction showed through the anger for a moment. Fuck. Pretty much the worst thing to do when Kira's mad is show weakness.

"I just flew three thousand miles only to find you goddamned lovebirds waiting at the other end. And you're telling me asswipe here didn't do it?"

Kira looked down at me, a vein twitching in her jaw. She was only a few inches taller, but god-*damn* did she use every inch to its fullest, most intimidating effect. I was suddenly *very* aware that I stood between her and the exit. Nonetheless, I stood my ground. If she wanted to walk out on us, she'd have to earn it. Especially after that *lovebirds* comment.

"I don't fucking believe you, Addie," she snarled. "I thought you were smarter than this. Why in cock-blasting *Christ*—"

Her fist slammed into the wall with a hollow *thud*. I winced at the dent it left and hoped who-ever'd paid for the room wasn't expecting their deposit back. At least Kira seemed a little calmer now.

"I haven't forgiven Jason," said Addie, calm in the face of Kira's rage-typhoon. "But in the interest of showing professionalism under the possible scrutiny of my employer, I intend to work along-side him *as an equal* until the job is done."

I had no doubt that she'd stressed the *equal* part as much for my benefit as Kira's.

"I just discovered Addie was part of this a couple hours ago," I said. "And neither of us knew you'd be here until you walked in."

"So we were just all coincidentally hired for the same job?" Kira's voice dripped with condescension.

"These things don't happen by coincidence," I said. "I think whoever's behind this knew *exactly* what they were doing."

"And they might not like you walking out now," Addie pointed out. "What did they give you? Fifty K in advance?"

Kira said nothing, which I took as a yes. The blotches of color were fading from her cheeks, but her brow was still thunderous.

"Yeah, they'll want their money's worth."

Kira flexed her fingers one by one, probably imagining how my neck would fit between them.

"I already made him promise to quit the bullshit . . . " Addie pressed.

"I'm all reformed," I said. "Thief's honor. I'm here to do the job, not rope you back in."

The world stopped on its axis as Kira mulled things over. Addie and I held our breath and watched.

"Fine, okay, I'll stay," she said at last, "on one condition: the plan doesn't involve me—"

But she cut herself off abruptly, slamming her mouth shut like a bear trap.

Addie frowned. "The plan can't involve you?"

Kira shook her head. "Never mind!" she said, suddenly sounding like her normal chipper self. I blinked, jarred by the change. "I'm good. Yeah, I'll do it. All the fun of the old gang, without any of Jason's bullshit? For a hundred-fifty K? It's like Christmas!"

Addie caught my eye. She was just as weirded out by Kira's sudden enthusiasm as I was. Unnoticed by Kira, a look passed between us, one that said, *Let's discuss this later.*

"Glad you're with us," said Addie. She looked

from me to Kira and then back at me again. "Now, the obvious question is, what are the odds that Z's team member number four?"

"I'm putting it at eighty-five percent," I said. "If our employer knows Kira was involved, he knows us all. And looking at our team so far, let's just say there's a pattern."

"Yeah . . . he's on a plane here right now, isn't he?" Addie's expression was unreadable, and I would've paid handsomely to read it, to know how she felt about the CPC reuniting once more.

Kira laughed. "Puh-leez. He probably missed his flight because the TSA had to confiscate all his shampoo . . . You know, that's not as fun when he isn't here."

"I'll tell him you said it," I promised sarcastically. "I bet he's been missing your verbal abuse. Keeps him up most nights crying, probably."

"I'll have to bring my A game then," said Kira. Every trace of her former angry self had vanished behind sunshine and rainbows at this point. It was too drastic a change—suspiciously so. I was *definitely* getting Addie's perspective later.

"Assuming he shows up," Addie pointed out. "It could be just us three."

"Wouldn't *that* be awkward," I chuckled. "If we just kept waiting, and then the game happened."

Addie shrugged. "Even then, we'd have a shot at getting paid, right?"

We all laughed at that. The atmosphere was suddenly infectiously cheerful. It reminded me of the old CPC meetings. I almost mentioned that—almost. But I held it back. Now wasn't the time, not when I'd *just* assured Kira that I wasn't gonna try and get the group back together permanently.

Can you blame me for planning just that, though? We *obviously* belonged together. And maybe I hadn't engineered our reunion, but I definitely wasn't above taking advantage of it.

Of course, it just wouldn't be the same if Z failed to show.

FOUR

"YOU THINK PEOPLE WON'T *NOTICE* THE SCOREboard isn't updating for Duke?" Z fixed Kira with a skeptical stare. "They're all paying attention. They aren't *stupid.*"

He had, in fact, shown up the very next morning. Predictably, he wasn't happy to discover that the elite team of criminal masterminds he'd been expecting were his pals from high school.

And me being one of those "pals" hadn't helped.

There'd been a shouting match, but he'd gotten over it eventually, just like the others. Again, it was mostly Addie's doing—she'd managed to calm him down and convince him I hadn't engineered this, which re-focused Z's anger on whoever *had*. Then Kira told him to "nut up and help," and Z said he would if I swore on the Bible not to hide anything from the group. Addie found the Gideon's Bible lurking in a dresser and I put my hand on it and swore. I felt awkward the entire time because Z was clearly taking it much more seriously than me, but once I'd finished, he settled right down. If I'd known it'd be that easy, I'd have done it weeks ago.

I'd break that promise the moment I needed to, but it'd reassured *them* just fine.

After tempers had settled and Z'd unpacked and organized his many shampoos, we convened around the table to collate our information and start planning. Z's e-mail had informed him that he'd be the last arrival, so we weren't waiting on anyone else. It was just us four. Again.

The job had officially begun.

"Alright, alright, jeez. Just an idea." Kira held up her hands in mock surrender. "But maybe there's something in it?"

"Nope," said Z. "Sorry."

But Kira wouldn't be deterred. "What if we shoved money into the Duke team's hands and told them to lose?"

It was Addie's turn to shoot Kira down. "The more people we involve, the more people can talk, and it'll only take one. Sure, we'd accomplish our goal of rigging the game, but our employers wouldn't be happy. We want to show them that we can be reliable and safe, as well as effective."

Z frowned at her from across the table—he still wasn't convinced we were being tested—but said nothing. It was too early to reopen *that* argument.

"Alright, I'm out," said Kira. "That's all I got. This shit's *hard*."

"If it was easy, everybody'd do it," I pointed out. "But we aren't everybody. We're the best, and we're gonna prove it."

The rest of the table completely failed to applaud, shed impassioned tears, or nod their heads solemnly. But that was *their* failing, not mine.

"Whatevs," said Kira. "I'm gonna get a soda. Anyone want anything?"

"Nah."

"Orange for me."

"Coke," said Z, Addie, and I, in that order.

"You got it!" said Kira, and withdrew. In her absence, the conversation turned to more serious matters.

"Dude, you know she's gonna bring back four root beers, right?" Z asked me. "She pulls this shit every time."

Serious is a relative term.

I smirked. "I prefer to humor her. There's no telling what could destabilize her." I could see Z had no idea what I meant, so I clarified. "Like, have you noticed how Kira—"

Addie shot me a *not now* look from behind him.

"—gets really mad when you don't play along with her dumb jokes?" I finished.

"Uh . . . not really?"

"Well, not mad, exactly, that wasn't maybe the right—"

"Forget it," said Addie, saving me. I resolved to thank her later. "Back to the plan. We can't bribe *everyone*, but maybe just one or two, ones we deemed safe risks—"

"I like it," said Z immediately. "I was thinking that too. If we bribed a guy to text us the team strategy, fill us in on the time-out huddles, we could—"

"We'd have to choose pretty carefully," I said. "Spying like that is a step above just playing poorly. Maybe someone *really* disgruntled . . . jealous of the star player?"

"We don't have *time,* is the thing," said Addie. "If we studied the group dynamic for a month, it'd be easier, but we can't. Let's not use the spy thing."

"If they aren't spying, just a couple players won't have a big enough impact," Z countered.

"Then we'll shoot bigger," I said. "What if we bribed the ref instead?"

Z rolled his eyes. "*Everyone* does that. It's like the most clichéd thing ever."

The sound of the door opening heralded Kira's return. "Sodas incoming!" she shouted from the hallway. Z looked at us mournfully.

"OK . . . a root beer for me," said Kira, plopping a can in front of her vacant chair. "Addie, yours was . . .?"

"Oran—"

"Root beer, I remember now!" A second root beer joined the first on the table. Addie pursed her thin lips, and Kira shook with suppressed laughter.

"And Jace, you ordered the root beer, right?" she said, sending a third can skidding across the table at me. I could already feel the beverage on my tongue, tasting like Coke-deprived disappointment. But if I didn't drink it, she'd win.

I couldn't allow that.

I popped the top, took a deep sip, and regretted it instantly. "Thanks," I managed.

"I guess that makes this one yours then!" Kira

continued, tossing her last can to Z, who caught it out of the air.

"But I said I didn't—"

"Now, what'd I miss?"

"I just suggested bribing the referee," I said, desperate to get the conversation back on track.

"And *I* said that's way too overdone," said Z immediately, looking like he wanted to go back to complaining about his root beer. I awarded him a mental gold star for not succumbing to his impulses.

"Maybe people do it because it *works.*" Some people just don't understand.

"But it's so *boring.*"

Before, I'd have swept his concerns aside, but I was on thin ice already. I'd been sitting back this meeting, taking a more passive role, even if it meant listening to Kira's inane ideas.

"Surely there's a compromise," said Addie, artfully stepping into the silence that followed my words. "Bribery will likely get the referee on our side, but that doesn't guarantee anything.

Remember, Maryland can't *just* win—we need a point spread of eight."

Z coughed. "*Point spread* refers to—"

"—The point differential between the teams, often used in sports bets to overcome the issue of people taking the low-risk route and betting on the favored team when presented with a simple win-lose binary."

I'd been waiting for the opportunity to show off my newly-acquired sports knowledge, and it was worth every second. Z looked like he'd been hit in the face with a pie, only to discover it was stuffed with olives. " . . . Yes. That."

He didn't have to know that my definition had been memorized almost word-for-word from a *Times* article I'd read only a couple days ago, or that I had basketball-themed flash cards in my suitcase's side pocket.

"*Anyway*," said Addie. "Bribery gives him room to work against us, or even go public. I say we remove that chance and go with blackmail. Have we considered that?"

"You know we haven't, you've been in the room this whole time," said Z. That smartass. *His* first instinct might be to downplay a good idea, but I was already pondering its applicability. I took another swig of root beer and winced as the anise met my tongue. "The only problem is, we'll need to find some dirt on the guy."

"No prob," said Kira immediately. "I'll dig up so much dirt, we'll all be in China."

"I still don't think one ref's enough to guarantee an eight-point spread. Duke's been kicking ass, and they're gonna bring their A game to the semifinals."

"You're probably right," I admitted. "But besides the ref, there's really just the players, and we talked about why bribing *them* won't be effective—"

"What about injury?"

I'm not sure what was more surprising—that Addie'd said that, or that it *hadn't* been Kira.

"Don't look at me like that. Taking out a few

of Duke's stars *and* blackmailing the referee would be enough, no problem. If we got Kira close to them and started a fight, she'd stomp them into the ground. You can thank me later, Kira."

There was a pause as we waited for Kira to wholeheartedly endorse this plan—it was, after all, *exactly* her style. She should've been bouncing off the walls in excitement.

And yet, the seconds stretched on . . .

"Well, shucks," she said at last, just as the silence was becoming awkward. "I—"

"Hold a minute," I broke in. "If Kira whales on a star basketball player, and then his team loses, it'll make news. Then comes the lawsuit, and that won't end well for *her*. You can't go around punching people these days. Kira, I'd want you backing me in a fight any day, but in a battle with the Las Vegas judicial system, you aren't gonna come out on top."

"Don't blame you there," said Kira. She drained her root beer, crushed the can between her fists, and tossed it into the wastebasket on the other side of the room, then reached for Z's untouched can. He made no move to stop her. "The courts fight dirty. Dirtier than me."

I didn't give Addie time to prepare a counter-argument. The group discussion had gone on long enough—it was time to remind everyone why they'd used to leave the planning to *me*. "We could come up with some foolproof plan that made the case impossible to solve, yes, but with a high-profile event, that shit starts conspiracies. People will *know* the game was rigged even if they can't prove it. However, if we make the fight more organic and spontaneous, it'll be that much easier to prosecute. It's a perfectly flawed plan, where compensating in one direction harms it in another. With me so far?"

They were.

"Luckily, keeping Kira out of the slammer's easy. She just needs to *not fight*. We don't need her to lay down the pain as long as the pain *is* being laid down. So we start a fight between Duke's shining star and a patsy. Then the law throws the book at *him* . . . and we're home free."

I paused for breath. Kira began a slow clap. "Ladies and dude, the Jason is *back*."

"Just one thing," said Z irritably. "I don't *manipulate crowds.* I make friends, and they do me favors."

"Yeah, yeah," I said. Z enjoys pretending there's a difference. Whatever helps him sleep at night. "So you guys like it, then?"

"Love it," said Kira emphatically. I wasn't sure why she was suddenly being so supportive (especially when I'd nixed her favorite part of the plan) but I wasn't about to look a gift horse in the mouth—I needed *one* source of solid support in this group. And I should've known it'd be Kira. We went back too far for a little spat to ruin our friendship forever. No wonder she was acting weird—who *wouldn't* behave differently when a good friendship was rockier than normal?

Anyway, my plan met with no opposition—if less enthusiasm—from Addie and Z, so we had our rough draft. And then, because staying in the group's good favor was still on my mind, I suggested we break for lunch.

"Sure," said Kira. "Planning's boring anyway."

"I'm looking forward to actually getting that orange soda," Addie said wryly, and Kira, laughing, grabbed *her* root beer too.

I clapped my hands once. "Then let there be lunch."

"Wait!"

Everyone looked at Addie, whose bright green eyes were sparkling with pride. "I just thought of something. We *could* just rig the game and be done. That would be *enough*. But what if we also stacked the odds? Say, if we intimated that the game was rigged . . . the other way?"

"Easy. If we gave people reason to believe a certain bet had a guaranteed yield associated with it, they'd take that bet, which would drive up Maryland's odds . . . and make the house a bunch more money. Thus impressing whoever hired us." It was such a good idea, I wished I'd thought of it first. "Contingent on us making the lie believable, of course."

"With Z masterminding it, the rumor would spread convincingly, right, Z?" asked Addie sweetly.

"I'm not gonna lie to my friends like that," Z protested.

Addie ignored him. "At the same time, it poisons the well against allegations of rigging when Maryland wins—the accusers will just look bitter."

"I think you missed me saying I wouldn't—"

"Yes you will, Z," I said firmly. "A professional would do it, and we're professionals now. Alright, it's part of the plan. Too bad we can't bet on it ourselves, huh?"

Even Z, who was making one of his angry faces again, looked saddened at the reminder. "Missed opportunity," Kira sighed.

As annoying as that clause was, it *had* confirmed for me that our employer had some connection to college sports betting, whether legal or otherwise.

That seemed the obvious subtext to the job, but you never know—it *could've* been an overzealous Maryland alum.

It also told me they were smart. That rule was obviously there to keep us from ripping off *their* organization—I didn't see why they'd care if we cleaned out a rival. But if they'd included a detailed list of acceptable betting venues, that would've made it easier to figure out which venue *they* were. And they obviously valued their anonymity.

When nobody else had any last-minute thoughts to share, we scattered to prepare for lunch. Kira made a beeline for the bathroom (three root beers will have that effect), Z began digging through his still-packed luggage for a clean shirt, and Addie slipped out to call the elevator. *I* pulled up a list of restaurants on my smartphone—when the inevitable argument began, I wanted to be prepared.

Kira caught up with me halfway to the elevator. "Hey," she said, giving me a wide smile.

I still wasn't sure what I should be prepared

for with Kira, smile or not. She *had* threatened me not twenty-four hours ago, after all, and my mental model of her was currently underperforming. "Hey," I said, hoping my own smile was the right response.

She lowered her voice then, looking very serious. "Thanks," she muttered awkwardly, like it was another language. "For, y'know."

I couldn't tell if this was another joke. "I do?"

"Back at the meeting," she prodded.

I looked at her helplessly and she stared back. I had no idea what response she was obviously waiting for. Then she gave a sudden, flippant laugh.

"You know! Drinking the soda I got you! You were the only one who did, you know? It made me feel helpful!"

It was the most transparent deflection I'd ever seen.

"Anytime," I said with a tight smile, and then we'd caught up with the others at the elevator, ready for our first group meal in a month.

FIVE

IF YOUR FRIENDS ARE ANYTHING LIKE MINE, DECIDING where to eat is a major point of contention. If I hadn't put my intellect to the task of figuring out a system of choosing, the tension might've split the group apart before we even got started. And I'm gonna share that tip with you, in the hopes that it revolutionizes your social gatherings the way it revolutionized mine. Once you know it, it's up to you whether to spread it far and wide, or hoard it for yourself.

It's beautiful in its simplicity. Each person gets a single veto. Then they take turns suggesting restaurants. If a restaurant is suggested and not vetoed, the group goes there. If the restaurant *is* vetoed, the game continues. No restaurant can be named more than once, and no member of the group can suggest a location twice in a row. Finally, a three-to-one against vote is effectively a free veto.

It's easy to learn, but the strategy takes years to master—and nobody can deny that it's completely fair, as long as you aren't incredibly picky and everyone ignores your opinion after you've blown your veto.

An Indian restaurant and a deli had been proposed and vetoed. The current proposal was a local hamburger joint called Monsterburger.

"Veto," I said, and Z gave me a contemptuous look. He and Kira had used their vetoes already, leaving Addie with the last. But Z should've known I'd shoot that down. Burgers are little grease sandwiches, and messy besides.

Addie eyed us craftily. She had the power to suggest whatever she liked now, but if she miscalculated and chose something we all hated, she'd be vetoed and forfeit the next suggestion. But if she thought about her choice too long, someone else might swoop in with something *she* wanted to veto. And veto-less scenarios can get chaotic.

"There's an Italian pasta place three blocks down," remarked Kira, reading off her phone. "That's my next shot. What'cha gonna do about it, girl?"

We stared at Addie expectantly. The corner of her mouth twitched as she basked in the power she now held over us. Finally . . .

"I'll allow it," she said, and Kira breathed a sigh of relief. Z, on the other hand, looked miserable. Kira bopped him on the head with the back of her hand.

"Play smarter next time, you baby."

Personally, I didn't mind—we'd managed to avoid Monsterburger (my arteries were clogging just thinking about it) and whichever weird, vegan, locally-sourced restaurants were native to the area.

Mr. Fermata's, as the restaurant billed itself,

looked okay. It was small, but it had an outside patio. A battered sign hung above the door, depicting a man who was either eating a musical note or holding up a fork while singing. Possibly both. It was nicer on the inside than the outside, which I suppose made sense from a practical standpoint, but likely didn't bode well for the future of the business unless it was generating some serious word-of-mouth buzz.

"I'm getting a weird inclination to check the menu and go somewhere else if the dishes are over ten dollars," muttered Addie. "Someone remind me I can afford stuff like this now."

"You can afford stuff like this now," I said. "Also, you're bound by the sacred rites of the restaurant game to eat here whether you can afford it or not."

"That too." Addie smiled ruefully. "Old habits die hard, I guess. I've only had more money than I needed for around a month."

"Are you trying to get out of credit card roulette, or volunteering to pay?"

"Those cancel out to the usual system, right?"

All eyes turned to me as the CPC procedure expert. Strictly speaking, I should've pointed out that CPC procedure didn't apply anymore, but why *remind* them if they were so willing to forget? We were coming together again faster than I'd hoped, and you could barely tell we'd been at each other's throats only yesterday.

"Implied statements carry no official weight," I said. "Although, if you *are* offering to pay . . . "

"I'm feeling wealthy, not generous."

"Fair enough."

"Just look at the clam spaghetti!" Addie said, jabbing her finger at the menu. "Twenty-six dollars. I can buy that. I can buy everything on the menu and sample it! . . . Not that I'd actually do that," she added hastily.

"I'll say. You know they'd hold our orders until all yours were done," said Kira.

"Besides, they'd all suck," said Z, who was still annoyed Italian had beaten burgers.

"*You* suck."

"Real original, Kira. You should have your own show."

"Hey. With the dosh I got from that poker game, I could buy one. Maybe I will. *The Kira Show.* Nonstop Kira, twenty-four seven."

"Yeah," countered Z. "And I could buy all the shits I wouldn't give about your dumb show."

"I could buy some new friends," I said. "Fresh new comebacks, twice as mature."

"'K." Kira tapped the table thoughtfully. "Addie buys more food than she can eat, Z buys a pile of shit, you buy friends—which most people can get for free, b-t-dubs—and I buy a TV show. Does that make *me* the smart one?"

Addie, Z, and I looked at each other in astonishment. "Fuck," Z said weakly.

Kira's face was frozen in an expression of utter joy, like she'd just gotten an entire toy shop for Christmas, but wasn't sure if it was all a prank and didn't want to celebrate in case it was taken away again. Not that she had to worry—as far as I was concerned, she'd won this round. Never let it be said that I don't admit defeat when I've been fairly trounced.

When nobody started laughing at her, she punched the air. "Yes!"

"Enjoy it while you can," said Z bitterly, reaching for the bread basket.

I've always disliked menus. Call it petty, but it's like they're mocking me with their plethora of options. There're hundreds of restaurants in visiting distance at any given time, and with each one's extensive menu, that becomes a cornucopia of possible meals with varying tastes, prices, and nutrition—and some of those variables are unknown until *after* you've picked. It's an optimization freak's nightmare. I finally settled on the wood-grilled duck, since it was the most unusual-yet-still-probably-tasty item on the menu. It wasn't half bad. But others were less lucky.

"It's so *thin*," said Z. He picked gloomily at his antipasto.

"What were you expecting, a steak?" Addie shook her head, exasperated. "I *did* warn you." She was already halfway through her spaghetti and still going strong.

I tried my best to comfort him. "Cheer up. After this, we can hit the casinos. You can get something there." I was rewarded with a begrudging smile, so I pressed on. "Dude, it sucks your meat came like that. Want a wing?"

Z heartily accepted.

"I hear they're pretty good at detecting fakes here." said Addie. "So that plan might be out."

"Nah, it's good," said Z between bites. "We just gotta go to the right place. See, I know a couple guys—"

"In *Las fucking Vegas*?"

"—who sell the best fakes you've ever seen outta their living room. Yeah, it's not a cool story. They moved out here, I kept in touch. Oh, and one was just visiting New York for spring break, but I met him at a beach party and we swapped numbers—"

"I don't even know why you're surprised," I said loudly over Z's incredibly boring story. "Oh right, you didn't know Z as long as we did. This is normal. After a while, you just accept it."

"He raah," said Kira around a mouthful of lasagna.

"Not that I'm complaining," I said quickly, because Z can get touchy about his friends sometimes, and I still can't tell what exactly sets him off. "Glad you could make it, Z."

"Well, my family didn't want me to," said Z between bites of chicken. "Dad especially. I had to sell it as a trip to see my uncle Mitch. Good thing Mitch is cool and said he'd cover for me as long as I visited him for a few hours. I can do that after the game, though."

He drained his water and started crunching on the ice.

I didn't feel any pressure to share my story—that

Lucas simply didn't care enough about my whereabouts to stop me.

"Good thinking," said Kira, and Z glowed a bit—hearing Kira praise Z is like finding a unicorn in your back yard. "I dodged that issue with some mockup paperwork and official-looking emails. Far as the family knows, I'm with the class on a field trip. Although . . . " she grinned. "That's not too far off."

"You guys didn't slow down one bit, did you?" I asked, and Kira winked.

"What, and be *normal*? Who wants *that*? Not me."

"We're not normal. We're the best in the business." I lifted my glass high. "And I'd like to propose a toast, in honor of our first day reunited. To good food and good company. To us."

I was laying it on thick, but as I've mentioned, we were coming together again so fast that I thought I could get away with it. And sure enough, the toast was echoed, glasses were raised, and big, happy smiles were exchanged. And among those smiling faces, looking right at me, was Addie's, as pretty as it'd always been.

I'd reluctantly given up on a possible *thing* between us after the split, but with everything going so well, and the uncharacteristic openness of her smile, I couldn't help but sit straighter in my chair. And in the magic of that moment—surrounded by friends, far from Lucas Jorgensen, with newly-sparked romance swimming in my thoughts—I saw the endless possibility of this latest job, if done well. The four of us together, like we were meant to be, getting offer after offer but only taking the jobs that interested us. Becoming big names in the underworld. Having our talents recognized.

Even Lucas would have to be impressed *then.*

The moment was interrupted by the waiter bringing the check. Wordlessly—for it was ingrained tradition—everyone placed their credit cards in the center. Addie, having won the restaurant-picking game earlier, swept them up and started shuffling.

"Alright, I admit it," said Kira. "We made the right choice. Totally. You guys're the best. I can't believe we ever split."

"I know I am," said Addie. "But you're pretty cool too."

She placed her hands behind her back and looked at me inquisitively.

"Three," I said, picking a number semi-randomly. Addie brought her hands back around and flipped up the first card, the second, then the third.

Kira scowled playfully. "Did I mention I hate every last one of you?"

As she shoved her card roughly into the black folder, I thought about mentioning Addie's skill at card manipulation, and how strange it was that the person selected to pay was the most ironic option of the four. But then, why would I ruin her fun like that?

SIX

JOBS CAN BE SPLIT INTO THREE DISTINCT PHASES. There's the Frame, where you plan everything. That'd been yesterday. Then there's the Op, where all the exciting stuff happens. Then comes the Revel—when you shake hands and split the loot (or make frantic plan Bs and scatter before the law catches you).

Today—Wednesday—marked the transition from Frame to Op, and I was at loose ends. With the plan hacked out, there wasn't much else for me to do. Z'd been out of the hotel since six in the morning, no doubt connecting with people he'd traded baseball cards with at a spelling bee twelve years ago during a trip to the Bahamas. Addie was out running an errand for Kira, who sat hunched over her laptop with her headphones in and a look of intense concentration stamped firmly over her face. But I had nothing to do but sip defiantly at the lukewarm root beer Kira'd brought me and check my fingernails for dirt every fifteen minutes. So far, they remained dirt-free. I'd been checking them for two hours.

A less scrupulous planner would've built weaknesses into the original plan so he could prove his worth by "solving" his own manufactured problems. That's what *Lucas* would've advised I do. But I take pride in my work, in making my plans as airtight as possible. And if I *was* bored, well . . . that was just a sign that everything was going perfectly.

But there had to be *something* I could contribute, something that I could do myself. Maybe find a way around the "no betting" rule.

"Yo, Jace?"

"Yeah?"

"Can you Google Isaiah Porter for me?"

So much for rest and relaxation.

"Sure. Anything specific you're looking for? And could you spell that?"

"I-s-a-i-a-h. Anything weird. Just do what you can, bruh."

Having delivered those incredibly specific and helpful instructions, Kira turned back to her computer. I sighed and typed *Isaiah Porter* into Google.

"Got something for you," said Kira. "Fourteen oh-one Wengert Avenue. That's not exact. Could be fourteen oh-three or thirteen ninety-nine."

I glanced over at her for clarification, but she wasn't looking at me. It took me a second to spot the headset she'd been speaking into.

Back at my own screen, several different Isaiah Porters competed for my attention. One was a football player, one was a senior editor for the *Las Vegas Sun*, and the third was studying anthropology at the University of Michigan.

"Awesome," said Kira in response to something I couldn't hear.

"It's the guy in Las Vegas, right?" I asked. I assumed that was the case, but being wrong would cost me a lot more than asking would.

"Huh?"

"Isaiah Porter. There are three of him. We want the one in Vegas?"

"Yeah. I mean, I assume." Kira frowned. "Sure, go with that."

"Alright. Just checking."

Over the next couple hours, I learned more about Isaiah Porter than I'd ever wanted to know. He was black, forty-nine, thin-faced, and usually clean-shaven. Among other factoids, I now knew he'd attended Brown University and written for their conveniently-archived school newspaper, in which he'd encouraged using DNA testing in criminal cases, advocated a cease-fire in Ireland, and covered numerous college sporting events. He'd moved on to work at the *Providence Journal* as a sports columnist. There was a six-year gap between his leaving the *Journal* and joining the *Sun*, but he'd obviously moved to Las Vegas between jobs. He'd also played a gambler in an amateur production of *Guys and Dolls*, but his acting career didn't seem to have taken off.

All very interesting, but I had *no idea what I was searching for.*

I didn't ask Kira again—there was no guarantee she'd be more helpful the second time, and she *did* look legitimately busy. Reluctantly, I resigned myself to my task and started skimming the web page of a church that advertised Isaiah Porter among its members.

"How are things back here?" asked Addie, and I jerked my head up, startled. I hadn't heard her come in.

"Don't *do* that."

"Sorry," said Addie, but she didn't look sorry at all. "How's it coming? Keeping busy?"

Kira grunted. Her headphones were dangling from around her neck.

"My mission was a wash," Addie said to her,

sitting down at the table. "It seemed like a normal house to me."

"Dicks," said Kira. "What about you, Jace?"

"Uh . . . " I knew Mr. Porter's political leanings (center-left), the names of his two children (Alice and Thom), and how many times he'd posted from his Twitter account (three), but I doubted any of that mattered. Would it *kill* Kira to tell me why this guy was important? I was starting to understand how everyone else felt around *me*.

"Looks like it's back to work for everyone," said Kira, oozing fake cheer in potentially lethal doses.

"Alright, but before I do, can someone *please* fill me in? House? What?"

Kira jerked her head towards Addie. "You do it. I'm busy."

"Fine, fine . . ." Addie got up. "Let's go into the other room so we don't disturb her."

I followed her toward—and then, to my surprise, *into*—the bathroom. Once I was inside, she closed and locked the door behind us.

"Alright," said Addie in a low voice. "We're finally alone."

It was *very* hard to tell where this was going when the only scenarios (alright, *fantasies*) I could imagine were of a singular nature.

"Let's figure out what's up with Kira, because she is acting *really* weird."

I scrambled to mask my disappointment, but I knew it was futile from the start. "Oh. *That.*"

"Yes, *that.* Why? Why else would I . . . never mind. Let's talk."

"Yes. So, Kira's acting strange," I said. "Stranger than normal. She went from super-mad to happy *really* fast. And it sounded for a moment like she wanted us to keep her off the mission."

Addie frowned pensively. "Doesn't sound like the Kira I know."

"It gets weirder," I said. "Kira and I talked right before we left for lunch."

"Wasn't that the planning meeting?"

"Between that and the elevator. She tried to thank me for something."

"What for?"

"Hell if I know. She just said 'thanks.' I had no clue why, and when she figured that out, she started laughing and made a joke about me drinking the root beer. But that's a heap of shit. She was thanking me for something else."

Addie's eyes were half closed in concentration. "Can you think of anything she could have meant?"

I sat down on the toilet. "All kinds of things. Just being *me*, for example. Being a standard for her to hold herself to."

Judging by her scowl, Addie didn't think much of *that* theory.

"But nothing immediately jumps to mind, no," I amended. "Like, why not just say why she was thanking me?"

We pondered this for a few seconds.

"She was acting weird at the meeting, too," I volunteered at last.

"Her cheerfulness isn't genuine," Addie agreed. "She's affecting the mood we expect, but she doesn't have it down perfectly."

"That's exactly it. Maybe she doesn't wanna be here, but she's trying to stay professional."

"That doesn't sound right, somehow . . . " said Addie. "Remember the meeting? I suggested she open a can of whoop-ass on some basketball player. I was trying to get her excited, but she froze up. When she finally said something, it sounded *really* fake—"

"But she's really absorbed in whatever she's doing *now*," I pointed out. "So she *is* enthusiastic about the job. Just . . . I dunno. This whole thing is weird and I don't have enough data for a hypothesis."

Sometimes, you have to admit you don't have enough information to solve the problem and resolve to come back later. This can be hard to do—I'm *still* struggling to get the hang of it. The English psychologist Peter Wason once ran an experiment where readers were asked to guess a mathematical rule.

They were allowed to test their guesses an unlimited number of times before they submitted their answer. Roughly eighty percent of respondents failed to adequately test their predictions, even though the cost of gaining information was almost zero. Often, people would rather be wrong than admit they aren't sure.

But it helps to remember that your confusion's temporary. You can always learn more and revisit the problem.

"Keep gathering data then," she said. "Kira's unstable, and I need to know why."

I didn't wanna go *that* far—Kira's one of the most stable people I know. Well, except for her violent tendencies and adrenaline addiction. "Maybe it's not a big deal. It seems like she's fine working with us, and she's not undermining the job, so—"

"Don't brush this off," said Addie sternly. Her voice dropped even lower as she knelt down, suddenly inches from my face. "We *can't* ignore unknown variables. If she snaps and ruins the plan . . . "

I wanted to tell Addie she was wrong. That Kira

might *seem* like a barely-restrained lunatic, and could sometimes go loose-cannon at inopportune moments, but that I'd known her for years and that she was saner than the average teenager.

But I didn't. Because she was right.

I'd never seen Kira like this before, which meant everything I *thought* I knew about her had to be re-evaluated. And if I brushed off Addie's concerns and the job went south because of it, it'd be my fault—and not only would our employer be mad, Addie'd *never* let me forget it.

So I forced myself to consider the possibility that something was very wrong with Kira.

"I'll keep a closer eye on her," I said at last. "The moment I get a clearer picture, I'll come to you."

"Same. Glad we could talk," said Addie. She put her hand on the doorknob. "I wanted it to be just us. Not Kira because *of course*, and Z, well, his thing for her might make it awkward depending on what—"

I just about choked to death on my own throat. "*Z* and *Kira*?"

Addie looked at me like I'd asked her what country we were in. "It's *so* obvious. Are you blind?"

"No way. For one thing—"

"He only agreed to stay after *she* asked him to," Addie pointed out. "Just watch for it, you'll see it. Trust me, this is what I'm good at."

"I trust you," I said slowly, trying to think back through all my interactions with Z and Kira. " . . . Well, fuck. Nobody tells me anything."

"I thought you knew." Addie shrugged, then opened the door. "Between you and me . . . it's never happening."

"Wait!"

Addie froze, then slowly swung the door shut again.

"Can you please *actually* tell me what's going on with the house and this guy Isaiah Porter?"

Addie blinked. "Right. Sorry. Kira somehow found who's reffing the Duke-Maryland game. That's him—Isaiah Porter. She sent me to look through his house and see if he was secretly dealing drugs or keeping children in his basement or something else we could blackmail him with. Didn't find anything."

Just knowing *that* clarified so much. "She had me tracing his online footprint all day. I guess she was hoping I'd find a scandal from his past or something."

But of *course* something like that would be buried deeper than a random Google search could unearth. If Kira'd only *filled me in*, I would've pointed that out and saved myself all that wasted work.

"You know," I continued, "if Isaiah has any skeletons in his closet—and that's still an *if*—they might take more than a couple days to dig up."

Addie chewed her lower lip thoughtfully. "Do we need a new plan?"

"Nah," I said, getting up from the toilet. "If we can't find a scandal, we'll just have to invent one."

SEVEN

AFTER A LONG DAY OF WORK, WHY NOT DECOMPRESS on the Strip?

That's what Kira'd *thought* I had in mind when I'd announced we'd be hitting up Treasure Island Casino that night. She certainly hadn't expected another few hours on the job, and when she learned the truth, I heard nothing but the word "bullshit" repeated at odd intervals and varying volumes for the next hour. I thought she'd stop when we flagged down our taxi, but it only redoubled her efforts.

I liked being in a taxi again. It reminded me of home. As long as I didn't look out the windows, I could pretend Las Vegas didn't exist. Of course, that meant looking at the cab's *interior*, which meant making occasional eye contact with Kira, which meant—

"Bullshit."

"I told you," I explained patiently. "We've got too much to do to goof off until Friday. We *need* to deal with Duke's team."

Kira huffed. "Yeah, but it's just recon tonight, right? You know I'm no good at that shit. You guys can stay on duty while I buzz off."

"No can do. I need you here just in case. This is one of those 'flexible' plans."

"Bull*shit.*"

Z'd discovered where Duke's team would be partying tonight through (what else) an old friend, whom he'd apparently met four years ago at a Bar Mitzvah. Luckily, he'd also found the time to secure our fake IDs, which he'd assured us would hold up to scrutiny if we were carded. Ideally, we wouldn't have to test that.

"Nancy'll meet me by the stack of treasure

chests near the arcade," he said, not looking up from his phone.

Addie saluted. "Gotcha."

I didn't want Nancy seeing us, in case we had to do something suspicious in front of her later. Z agreed, though he made it sound like he was ashamed to be seen with me. But the important thing's that we *did* agree, never mind the why and wherefore, so the rest of us were going in first, planting ourselves at the meeting point, then lurking near Nancy and Z and absorbing as much of their conversation as possible. Addie was going because she could effortlessly blend with the crowd. *I* was going because I wanted firsthand experience with the information I'd be sculpting a plan with later. And since I couldn't go unnoticed like Addie, I needed Kira along to have a fake conversation with.

She was right that she was mostly extraneous to this particular mission, but like all good moves, bringing her served an ulterior purpose—I was hoping to keep her away from the slots. Kira's exactly the kind of person these casinos target, and the *last* thing I needed was her losing twenty thousand dollars and making a scene. I'd made her promise not to gamble before we left, but I knew *that*'d last until she learned drinks were free as long as you were spinning slots. And *then* she'd lose money to a machine, her competitive streak would kick in and she'd ride the adrenaline of each spin all the way to bankruptcy.

She could do that in her *own* time.

"See y'all inside," said Z as we piled out of the taxi and promptly wilted beneath the intense heat of the Strip. Las Vegas apparently didn't believe in nighttime, because it was almost as bright and warm as it'd been four hours ago. I was lost in a sea of glitter and neon, all of it competing for my attention. This was the City of Sin in its element, thriving off the teeming mass of pilgrims that ebbed and flowed along the streets like a tide.

Kira pushed past me, squared her shoulders, and waded in. The crowds parted before her and we followed in her wake. Soon, concrete gave way to boardwalk beneath our feet, and then boardwalk to carpeting as we passed through the enormous double doors.

Addie took point once we were inside, looking around for the chests. It took a few secondhand directions from Z, but she was eventually able to lead us right to them, at which point she vanished among the milling tourists.

"You catch the lagoon outside?" said Kira. "Shit was *real*."

I hadn't, hemmed in by bodies as I'd been, but I knew Kira'd laugh at me for being short if I admitted it. Which is bullshit, since she's not even that much taller than me, but that's never stopped her. Instead, I just agreed. "Yeah. Though *real* isn't the word I'd use."

We didn't have to wait long—a tall, dark-haired girl-slash-woman detached herself from the crowd and embraced Z, who greeted her enthusiastically. I edged Kira towards them subtly, but I needn't have bothered, because they headed towards the slots almost immediately. Kira gave one a look-over and I tensed, but she stayed with me . . . for now.

"*Tits*, I'm tired," she complained. "Been working on this Isaiah Porter thing all day. Just back and forth between Photoshop and that stupid newspaper's records. I've seen enough spreadsheets for *years*. I thought I deserved a little break. I thought you'd see things my way. But here I am, *still* working my ass off—"

"Yeah, and you got to sit down the whole time," I pointed out. "Z's been on his feet twelve hours, and you don't hear *him* complai—well . . . he does it. And that's something."

"Well, you know how the saying goes. All work and no play makes Kira wanna knock heads."

She gave me a sidelong look as she said that, the look she gives whenever she's searching for a reaction . . . which is most of the time. So I played my part and sighed loudly, because she'd sulk if I didn't. "That's not how it goes."

Nancy was waving over a beefy, blond-haired

man who I assumed was her boyfriend. Actually, most of the people in this area were athletic college-aged men. It was almost bereft of adults altogether, except for one old man with a giant gray mustache who appeared to be their coach, and one guy doggedly playing the slots next to (and steadfastly ignoring) a very touchy-feely couple. If I squinted, he looked kinda like the popsicle vendor who always set up his stall outside Van Buren, even in the winter. I pointed him out to Kira—"Popsicle dude, right?"—and she laughed.

We used the pretense of being interested in him to get closer to Nancy and Z, but they weren't saying anything interesting—just introductions. Nancy kept calling over identical, cookie-cutter jocks—some of whom Z already knew—but eventually, the flow dried to a trickle, and the conversation turned to more relevant matters. Z was in his element, subtly but deftly steering the discussion towards the team and their strategies. I kept my ears pricked and drank in every word. Some stuff got lost in the noise, but Z was really good about repeating or paraphrasing things in a loud, carrying voice for me, so I followed everything well enough. It was easier than it could've been, mainly because it kept circling back to one common element—Brett Tarquin, power forward for the Blue Devils.

I had to read between the lines, but it was clear that if Jesus Christ came back down to Earth as a basketball player, he'd still lose a game of HORSE to Brett Tarquin. He'd made MVP two years running, and everyone agreed he'd take it home again this year. My recently-acquired basketball knowledge was *just* enough for me to appreciate their stories about him.

He was Duke's linchpin, their ace in the hole. Naturally, he had to be removed.

In answer to a question of Z's, Nancy pointed towards the bar. I just followed her finger and there he was—Brett Tarquin. In the flesh.

He was handsome, no denying that. The women he'd captivated certainly didn't. As I watched, he threw his arm around one and waved the bartender over while the others pouted.

"He's *such* a player," giggled Nancy. Her tone, a touch more admiring than admonishing, didn't go unnoticed by her boyfriend, and his face darkened imperceptibly. Like every other piece of information I'd gathered, I filed it away . . . but it was unimportant for now.

Brett, though . . . *that* had potential. I was already weaving a plan out of the individual threads of information that'd come my way so far. But the more thread I had to work with, the better the final product would be.

I walked casually over to the bar, flashed my fake, and ordered a rum and coke, listening through my left ear and sneaking glances whenever I could conjure an excuse. It wasn't a task that required my full attention—Brett was an open book. He was brash and shameless, with an entitlement complex a mile wide . . . an inevitability with a team that sycophantic.

And then I glanced over my shoulder at them and got a good look at Brett's face. He was wearing the same self-confident smirk I usually associate with Lucas, but on a face thirty years younger.

I imagined *him* sitting on that stool—a little less muscled, with darker hair, but still with that same damnable smirk—and the plan fell into place almost immediately. I knew *exactly* how to deal with people like Brett Tarquin. I'd been doing it all my life.

I tilted my head back, finished my drink, and got up from my stool. As far as I was concerned, Brett's smirk had told me everything I needed to know. Time to rejoin Kira—except Kira wasn't where I'd left her. My heart sank as I realized where she'd probably gone.

"She went that way," said Addie from my left.

I started at her sudden appearance, then immediately felt silly "How long've you *been* there?"

"Not *that* long," said Addie, looking pleased

with herself. "Z's conversation got boring so I came to find you instead. You're only boring *sometimes*."

"You want not boring? Come help me rip Kira away from the slots before she sells a kidney. Not necessarily hers."

Addie paled. "Oh no. Oh *no*. She totally would."

We pushed our way through the casino, fearing the worst. Thankfully, Kira hadn't gone far—she was a few aisles down, just past a pirate-costumed barbershop quartet singing shanties to passers-by.

"*Kira*," I said, marching over, but she was already getting up. Addie and I shared a look of relief—we'd been prepared for a fight.

"All done," she said. "Let's make like a basketball and bounce."

My confusion must've registered as something else to her, because she looked at me and creased her forehead in a frown. "Don't judge. Like I was gonna come to Vegas and not try the slots."

"And you . . . tried them?" As always, Addie hid her surprise better than I ever could.

Kira shrugged. "A couple times. I don't see what the fuss is about. You pull a lever and then your money's gone. I heard it'd be *exciting,* but it's a boring-as-fuck piece of shit. Biggest letdown of my life. You were right, dude." She shook her head regretfully. "I should've stayed away."

I cleared my throat. "Um. Yes. That's what I was afraid of."

Addie was already walking back the way we'd come, but I called her back. "I think I got everything I need."

"Yeah?"

"Yeah. Their game revolves around Brett Tarquin, right? With him gone, the whole team crumbles. And I know how to deal with Brett Tarquin."

Kira smiled like a wolf and I shook my finger at her. "Not like that. This is *much* better."

If the Isaiah Porter operation went half as well as this, the job was as good as done.

EIGHT

THURSDAY. MORE SPECIFICALLY, LATE AFTERNOON. The day before the big game. Time was ticking down faster than I'd anticipated, and we were struggling to match the schedule. Kira'd finished her preparations only an hour ago, and I, again left to my own devices, had spent my time putting together a contingency plan or two. At five o'clock sharp, we were ready to begin the next phase of the plan.

Isaiah Porter's house was relatively small and painted white. Like every other house on the block, it had a small yard and a one-car garage. There was a car parked in the driveway—I wasn't sure if there was a second in the garage, but either way, *someone* was home. And given that Isaiah was by all accounts unmarried, it was probably him.

"It looks different when I know I'll be knocking," muttered Addie, and Kira grinned at her. We'd decided all three of us should be involved in the conversation (Z was again elsewhere, doing his own thing).

"No, really," she said. "I didn't even look at the front the first time, I accessed the backyard through the gate. They've got a basement entrance under the back porch, so I . . . nobody cares, huh."

"You done yet?" asked Kira, giving a large mock-yawn. "I think I dozed off for a sec."

She winked at Addie, then sauntered ahead of us, black briefcase swinging from her hand. She'd insisted on carrying it, and given the hours she'd spent crafting the contents, I'd decided she deserved it.

"Think this'll work?" I asked Addie as we followed Kira up the sidewalk. We didn't have briefcases, but we were no less professionally dressed—we were wearing matching black jackets, with Addie in a narrow, knee-length gray skirt and non-functional spectacles, and myself in sensible black slacks and a patterned green tie. Kira's pinstriped pantsuit was a fashion disaster (not to mention part of Lucas's "Dress for Success" clothing line, which I'd always hated), but at least we'd managed to talk her out of her usual T-shirt/jeans combo.

"If it doesn't, we'll have to come up with something else *really fast,*" she said. "This was *your* idea. Do *you* think it'll work?"

"There's no way to be sure, but as plans go, it's one of mine, so . . . yeah, we'll be fine."

"That's the spirit."

The yard was surrounded by a low, red-brick wall, and the lawn had seen better days. Together, they formed an impression of brownness around the house's white walls. Not a good look.

Kira awaited us on the doorstep. "Ready?" she asked, fist hovering by the door. The two of us nodded in unison. On the fourth knock, the door opened.

After seeing what felt like *hundreds* of pictures of the guy, I felt uniquely qualified to determine that this was, in fact, Isaiah Porter. He looked a little older, a little less photogenic, but there was no mistaking that forehead.

"Mr. Porter," I said, just to let the others know we had the right guy.

"Can I help you?" he asked.

"Hi!" said Kira, flashing him a bright grin. "We're with the *Sun.* We'd like to talk with you."

Isaiah's brow wrinkled. "I haven't ever seen you at the office."

"Yeah, we're not part of the, uh, office group—"

"Different branch," said Addie, cutting in and saving Kira, who thankfully stopped talking at once. "We handle legal affairs. Mind if we step in?"

I could see the wheels turning in his head as he regarded us, and I hoped we looked innocent and non-threatening, not like the kind of people who were looking for an excuse to come inside so we could rob him.

Because we'd *never* do that. Blackmail, sure. Not steal.

He shook his head in disbelief, suddenly coming to his senses. "You're just a couple kids."

I stepped forward and adopted my driest tone of voice. "I assure you, our youthfulness is no great impediment to our expertise. We are here on a matter of official business, Mr. Porter, and my colleagues and I will not be dissuaded. If you refuse to converse with us, you will be forced to settle for someone a good deal older *and* a good deal angrier, so I would recommend you cooperate."

Isaiah blinked. I'd hit him with a regular word whirlwind, and now he wasn't sure *what* to think.

"Just a quick chat," said Addie. "We'll be out before you know it."

She gave him a warm, beatific smile, and it

was basically over after that. You'd need a heart of stone to resist that smile.

"Come on in," said Isaiah, opening the door a little wider.

I don't mean to be judgmental of those in harsher circumstances, but walking into that house, you could *tell* print media was dying.

Isaiah ushered us into the living room and gestured to an old, ripped couch with several books and loose papers taking up one of the cushions. While we figured out who got to sit, he brought over a pair of wooden chairs and arranged them around the coffee table. "Can I get you anything to drink?" he asked.

"Root beer for me," said Kira.

"We'll be fine," said Addie, shooting a sharp look at Kira. "No drinks, please."

Kira and Addie sat on the couch. I took one of the chairs. Isaiah took the other.

"Now," he said. "To what do I owe the pleasure?"

I nodded at Kira, who opened her briefcase and pulled out a large folder.

"It has come to our attention, Mr. Porter," said Addie, "that there are a few irregularities in the *Las Vegas Sun*'s accounts. Money has been budgeted and reported used, but our account statements don't match the reports. In short, money is going missing, and we need your help locating it."

To his credit, Isaiah looked extremely concerned at the idea of foul play inside the company, like the thought hurt him on a personal level. I felt a sudden stab of guilt. Like, I'd signed off on the plan, but I'd expected Isaiah to hate his job just like everyone else. Knowing he was loyal to the company changed things. Was there a way to skip this step?

There are two kinds of people in this world. Lucas's voice echoed in my head. *The winners, and the compassionate. Mercy holds you back. You cannot win unless you operate at full capacity . . . and I can promise that in your place, they would not extend that mercy to* you.

Every day for *years* I heard that shit. You'd have trouble expunging it from your head too, I bet. At this point, I usually just tune it out, but this time was harder. Because I knew, as much as hearing Lucas's voice made me wanna do the *opposite* of whatever he was advising, that I had to stick to the plan. There wasn't time to withdraw and make a new one.

And yeah, as much as admitting this sucked, I *did* value myself and my friends over Isaiah Porter. Our futures were on the line, both individually and as a group. That was worth causing some discomfort.

"For example," said Addie. She paused, eyes scanning the contents of the folder. She sat perfectly straight on the dilapidated couch, looking every inch the young solicitor. "This irregularity here. United Airlines ticket to San Jose Airport for a Mr. Isaiah Porter. Ticket receipt, one hundred ninety-two dollars. Money reported spent, three hundred sixty-three dollars. Quite a difference, don't you agree?"

Isaiah was looking back and forth between us, aghast and disbelieving all at once. "Listen, I bought that ticket and—"

"Item two," said Addie, somehow drowning him out. "Isaiah Porter's interview dinner with Mr. Glenn Greenwald. Check, fifty-six dollars, thirty-two cents. Money reported spent, eighty-four dollars, twenty-one cents. Item three. Cost of ticket for—"

"Stop," said Isaiah. "There's something funny going on here."

Kira, smiling sweetly, handed him a stack of papers from her dossier, and his eyes widened in shock.

"Item three," Addie repeated. "Ticket for Cirque de Soleil, to be reviewed by Isaiah Porter. Ticket stub—"

"Stop it," said Isaiah, cutting her off again. "Just

stop. I get the picture. But look, there's got to be a mistake. I know what it looks like, but there's been a mistake. I never did it. I never did any of it. I remember all these things, but it's a mistake."

Addie bored right into his eyes with her own and didn't even twitch. "The *Las Vegas Sun* is taking this very seriously, Mr. Porter."

"I didn't do it," Isaiah repeated, ashen-faced. "Please, you've gotta believe me."

"Actually, Mr. Porter," I said, "we *do* believe you."

He turned to me, now confused out of his wits.

"Unfortunately," I said. "It's not us you have to convince. It's the *Sun*. We haven't made this discovery public yet, but it's all there, in the company files, waiting to be found. And trust me, you don't want that."

That wasn't, strictly speaking, true—Kira hadn't been able to change the archives from off-site—but I doubted he'd call our bluff.

"But I didn't do it," said Isaiah softly. "I'm no crook."

"You didn't," I said. "But it'll look like you did. Unless we change the records back, erase all evidence of your wrongdoing. Then, my friend, you're in the clear."

I could see the moment when the pieces fell into place, when the confusion in his eyes faded into betrayal . . . and then anger.

He hadn't asked for us to come in here and blackmail him. His only crime was serving a company faithfully for years, and now he saw the possibility of everything he'd worked for evaporating. It was almost enough to get me apologizing.

So I imagined Lucas sitting there, realizing what deep shit he was in, and a smirk spread across my face.

"I'll tell them it was you that did it," said Isaiah firmly.

I laughed. "You'll tell them what? Mr. Porter, you have no idea who we are. You're gonna tell the

Sun's lawyers that three *kids* framed you? They not only won't believe you, they'll be insulted that you think they're that stupid."

Isaiah stiffened.

"Look, it's not all bad," I said. "We don't want you fired, or jailed, or . . . anything. We're just as eager as you are to bury this. We just need one small favor first, and then your problems are over. Promise. You know what this is about, right?"

Isaiah slowly shook his head. Too slowly. I could tell he'd thought about saying yes.

"Don't pretend you aren't the referee for the upcoming NCAA game," I said. "We know you are. We're big basketball fans, and we're really looking forward to watching this game. You might even say we have a special interest in it."

Melodramatic, yes, but the goal was to make an impression.

"Is this some kind of joke?"

"I know you don't have the power to single-handedly throw the game in Maryland's favor, but that doesn't mean I don't want you to try your very best," I said.

"We understand," said Addie, "that you must remain plausibly impartial. But remember, *we* decide whether that plausible impartiality is spilling too far over into *actual* impartiality. And if we don't like what we see, your financial records go straight to your boss."

"Do we understand each other?" I asked. Man, Addie and I were on *point.* We hadn't even rehearsed this.

"If not," said Addie, "I'd like to introduce you to my friend, Miss Phoebe."

This was Kira's cue to give her best, most bloodthirsty smile. She'd been sitting off to the side this whole time, wearing a sweet, innocent look. Kira can do sweet and innocent pretty well if you don't know her, but her murder-smile is a fast window into what lies beneath the facade. Her pupils widened, her lips curled mockingly, and her teeth bared.

"Phoebe's a big fan of the Terrapins," said Addie. "She'll be crushed if they lose. And when Phoebe gets crushed by something, people tend to get crushed by *her*."

Isaiah's mouth opened and closed on nothing, searching desperately for words that wouldn't come.

"It's a big decision, and you need time," I said. "We'll let you think in peace. You won't be seeing us again, so if you choose to help us, make sure we can tell."

I rose, which was the signal for the other two to rise as well. As one, we moved toward the door. I turned on the doormat and gave the still-speechless journalist a formal bow.

"Thank you, Mr. Porter, for your time and hospitality."

And with that, we left. The cab was still waiting as we'd instructed—and still running the meter, of course, but it was nothing we couldn't afford.

We had to meet Z downtown in an hour, and we didn't have time to call another cab.

I still felt guilty as we pulled away from the curb. Kira was uncharacteristically quiet and I wondered if it was bothering my companions too. And if it'd gotten to *us* . . .

"Good thing Z didn't come," I said out loud, trying to gauge their reactions.

"Huh?" said Kira. "You mean because they're both—"

"Because he gets weird about screwing over innocent people, dumbass."

Lucas would say there *are* no innocent people. Screw or be screwed. But he's wrong—some people just wanna be left alone. And some are genuinely good people, like Isaiah Porter. In an ideal world, people like me could let them be—but then, if this world were ideal, *everything* would look different.

Kira just laughed. "What a cockblock."

The cab bounced along the pothole-scattered suburban road.

"You think he'll go for it?" Kira asked abruptly.

"I got that impression, but I can't read the future," I said. "We'll know for sure by Saturday, one way or the other. Then we'll all go out for drinks . . . or start packing our things and getting new identities."

I meant it as a joke, but there was something solemn about the weight of the words. Because the truth was, we still didn't know who'd hired us. We didn't know how forgiving they'd be if their advance payment ended up being squandered.

We didn't know if failure was even allowed.

THE RENDEZVOUS POINT WAS A TRENDY BAR called the Kosmos Lounge. Z'd been hanging out with Nancy and the boys for the past few hours, and they were ready to party it up—despite their coach's edicts, not to mention state drinking laws.

Addie pointed out that we couldn't show up to a place as hip as the Kosmos Lounge in business attire, so we detoured to Hollister to pick up something a little more casual. The goal was to blend in, after all—if we stuck in anyone's mind, we'd done something wrong.

In most cities, bars would be at least a little more

subdued on Thursday night. Not in Las Vegas—the Kosmos Lounge was packed to the gills with all manner of interesting-looking people. Funnily enough, every last one of them looked *exactly* like the kind of person you'd expect to find in a Las Vegas bar or club on a Thursday night.

At least it wasn't deserted. That would've complicated the plan—we would've had to fill the club with bodies, *then* start the fight. And in a worst-case scenario, I'd just've had Kira do it and minimized the consequences later.

Something itched in the back of my head, something I was missing. My brain apparently thought the idea of Kira starting the fight was important. Why, though? Because she was acting odd? But the feeling faded as quickly as it'd come and I filed it under *things to worry about later*. In a building this crowded, it was best to keep all the wits you could spare about you at all times.

Z's fakes again proved their worth at the door. The bouncer gave them a cursory glance, just long enough to make sure we hadn't handed him a lump of dog shit instead of an ID, and waved us along. I got the impression from his blank look that we might not've even needed the fakes at all.

As soon as we walked in, we were hit by the heat of a thousand tightly-pressed bodies. And the smell wasn't improving matters. It was like a dozen sweaty robots had vomited cheap vodka all over the room.

"Let's do this job really, really quickly," I muttered to Addie, but it got drowned out by a grating techno beat. Apparently, you needed a full-fledged outdoor voice if you wanted to be heard here. Because conversation's . . . for squares, I guess?

"What?"

"Never mind."

We pushed our way through the mass of patrons until we found a relatively open area at the far end of the bar.

"This would be easier with less people," I said,

huddling close so we could hear each other. "But I think it can still work."

"Fewer," said Addie, and I rolled my eyes. "It'll be harder in some ways, but easier in others. Once the fight gets going, it'll snowball."

Personally, I wasn't convinced that was a positive. "Remember, we aren't trying to start World War Three, just knock Brett on his ass."

"Can't see a fucking thing," said Kira, poking her head out of our huddle. "Too many people."

"Tilt your head up a little," I advised. "We're looking for the big ones."

The plan was almost insulting in its simplicity, and it involved those time-worn instigators of conflict—an attractive girl and a large, jealous boyfriend.

We spent a few minutes in silence, watching the milling crowd and—in my case—wrinkling my nose at the silver, space-age decor. The tables looked like they'd come straight out of the *Star Wars* movies. And not the good three, either.

It took four false alarms (half turned out to be single, and the other half didn't look mean or big enough), but we finally had a boyfriend picked out. He was six inches taller than even Kira, and his default expression—at least, what I *assumed* was his default expression—made him look like a Klingon sucking on a lemon.

"Look how his eyes keep flicking towards her," Addie pointed out. "He's cagey, threatened by the way she's smiling at other guys. And she sees it. She's playing it up just to piss him off. Yeah, this relationship won't last if he doesn't lighten up."

Took the words right out of my mouth, the showoff.

"What's Z up to?" I asked.

Kira—who'd been keeping in contact with Z—looked up from her Jägerbomb. "He got here a few minutes ago," she said. "He's ready when we are. He says Brett seems pretty fucking thirsty. And lemme tell you, I don't blame him. Some of the guys in here—"

"Focus on the job," said Addie sharply.

"Whatever," said Kira, turning back to her drink. "Hey, you want something?"

"If I do, I've got more than enough in the bank to afford it myself," said Addie, but she was smiling in spite of herself.

I looked toward the entrance, trying to spot Z, and finally saw him through a rare gap in the crowd. He stood in the middle of a small group of athletes, enthralling them with some funny story or other. He may be a sanctimonious asshole most of the time, but he's damned good at what he does, and I'll never deny it. Except to his face.

"Anyway, I'm up," said Addie. "Thanks, though."

She got up from her red leather-topped stool and slithered through the crowd toward the meathead we'd picked out. I could barely (or was that *almost?*) make out her bright "hi!" to his girlfriend. Personally, I'd be weirded out if a random stranger started talking at me in a bar, but Addie'd assured me that she could make it work.

With the pieces in place, there wasn't too much to do besides helicopter over Z and Addie, and I knew both of them would grouse at me later if I did, so I plopped myself down on Addie's vacated stool next to Kira.

"'Sup," she said, glancing towards me.

I eyed the empty glass next to her current half-full one. "You thinking of slowing down?"

"What, me? C'mon, Jace," Kira chuckled. "We've known each other four years now. Have I ever slowed down? Name one time. I bet you fucking can't."

I searched for a way to acknowledge her point while using it to back up my argument and failed.

"Yeah, that's what I fucking thought." She took another long drink. "Booze helps, you know?"

"Helps what?"

"You know," said Kira flippantly. "Good plan, by the way. I like it."

"Even though you aren't doing the actual punching?"

"Ha!" Kira laughed. "Yeah, I reckon I'll make it through somehow. There'll be other faces to bash in."

"That's the spirit," I said, patting her on the back. The bartender swept her tip off the counter and gave her an appreciative smile. Had there been a *twenty* in that wad of bills?

"Hey, did you mean to—"

"Oh, yeah," she said, waving a hand a little too exuberantly. "I've got so much fucking money, dude. I don't even know what to do with it. I figure if I can make that guy's night, that's good enough. I just . . . " her voice trailed off as she struggled to find the words. "You know," she said again.

I didn't—again—but even at her most coherent, Kira didn't make too much sense, and she was several drinks past *coherent* right now. "Yeah, I know."

Kira looked at me significantly, and now I was more confused than ever. Luckily—or maybe unfortunately—she changed the subject. "So, uh, how's things with Miss Sneaky? Getting in there?"

"Are you still on this? Look, my position's precarious enough as is. I want this job to go *right*. If I make things awkward and the group implodes and we fail, that's on me. So no. Not 'getting in there.'"

"Gotcha," said Kira, giving me an impressive side-eye. "Once the job's over, is what you're saying."

"I'm not saying—oh, shut up. Finish your drink."

"You're the boss," said Kira, amiable as ever. She picked up her glass and downed the rest in one big sip. "Bartender!" she called, lifting it triumphantly.

"No," I said firmly. "I'm cutting you off. I need you sharp so you can watch my back if things get ugly."

Kira glowered mutinously, but at least she lowered her glass. "You owe me big time."

I snorted. "For what, doing your job?"

"My job. Right."

My phone buzzed in my pocket—a text from Addie: incoming.

A few seconds later, Addie came pushing towards us, hand-in-hand with her new friend. "Hi guys!" she said brightly. "This is Jenna, my classmate from when we were tiny! Jenna, these are my friends from school!"

I would've bet my entire bank account that (a) Addie'd never met Jenna in her life, and (b) Jenna was over four years older than her. But Jenna seemed perfectly happy with Addie's version of events, so why point that out?

"Hi, Jenna!" Kira and I said in unison.

"Nice to meet you," said Kira, offering a wavering fist bump. "Name's Ki . . . ana."

"Ralph," I added quickly, trying to take attention off Kira, who was glaring at me for having kicked her in the leg.

"Her boyfriend's in the bathroom right now, so I thought I'd bring her over!" said Addie. "She's really cool. We haven't seen each other in like, five years! Crazy, right?"

As she said this, Kira slid me her phone surreptitiously. There was a message from Z: omw

"Here for the game?" Jenna asked me.

"Well, yeah," I said. "I'm a big fan. But I'm also here to see the sights."

"The sights are great," Kira interjected, waggling her eyebrows suggestively. Jenna tittered.

"Excuse me!"

Brett Tarquin himself had arrived, with his cadre (and Z) in tow. Z caught my eye and winked.

"Scotch on the rocks," said Brett to the bartender. "And for the lady, an Appletini. Unless she wants something stronger."

He didn't even look at Jenna, but there was no doubt he meant her—Z'd planted the bait well. Jenna flushed as she noticed him, and he took the opportunity to slide into the open area next to her, which had been occupied only seconds ago by Addie.

"But aren't you a sight for sore eyes," he said

with a cocky grin. "I was starting to think all the hotties had stayed in tonight."

Jenna giggled again. It got a little less endearing every time. "Are you saying I'm the cutest girl in here?"

"Don't get puffed up about it," said Brett. "But it is what it is. What do you say? Cutest girl, hottest guy? Destiny, right?"

I cast a quick glance at the bathroom and hoped for our sake there was a line. Brett didn't have much time to make an impression.

"I have a boyfriend," said Jenna, but her body language told a different story.

If there'd been any chance of Brett giving up, it vanished then. As I said before, I know how people like him work, and one thing they cannot abide is a "no." Telling them something's off-limits is a surefire way to make them want it.

Some of this comes from nobody telling them "no" in their everyday life, but a whole lot of it springs from their ego. A friendly challenge, like the kind Z had issued to get him over here, is usually enough to get them going. But Jenna had issued a challenge too, in her way, and Brett was suddenly playing for stakes. I could see his focus narrow, his posture shift.

"I have a pet cat, as long as we're talking about things that don't matter."

"*Damn,*" said Addie, looking at Brett with wide-eyed appreciation. "Jenn, are you really gonna say 'no' to that?"

I *knew* she was only acting, but that didn't stop a spike of jealousy from worming its way into my thoughts.

"Oh, I don't know," said Jenna, giving Brett a coy look.

"Limited time offer, babe," said Brett. "I'm in town for March Madness. I'm playing. Brett Tarquin, power forward." He said that last bit like it was some kind of lady-killing kryptonite. In all fairness, it worked.

"You're *playing*? What team?" Jenna looked genuinely interested now.

I looked back toward the bathrooms. Sure enough, Mr. Meathead was just outside the door, looking around the club. But Brett had somehow, maybe instinctively, positioned himself between him and Jenna, and the crowd made a thorough search impossible.

" . . . Got that pussy on lock," I heard one of the other players mutter to Z.

" . . . Just tell him you had a headache and left early."

"Oh yeah, Jenn!" said Addie with her own annoying little giggle. "I'll back you up. I can be your wingwoman!"

She gave Jenna a small shove towards Brett, who was looking immensely pleased with himself.

"Well, you *do* need a proper Las Vegas welcome," said Jenna slyly, picking up her Appletini. Then her brow wrinkled. "But my boyfriend—"

"Oh, he's an asshole, Jenn! You know that!" Addie was hitting it out of the park.

I looked back at Z to signal him to guide Meathead in this direction, but he was already gone. His instincts had told him shit was about to hit the fan.

"Alright," said Jenna. "I'm the basketball hoop and you're trying to score. Think you can make a three-pointer?"

"If I'm scoring on *you*, I'll make it a fucking four-pointer."

I didn't see them move—I must've blinked at the wrong time or something—but Brett and Jenna were suddenly making out like their lives depended on it.

"One relationship, ruined in the name of the job," I muttered to Kira, who was watching in tipsy fascination.

"Wooo! Get it, Jenn!" Addie cheered, while Brett's friends made loud congratulatory noises. Nobody thought to look elsewhere—nobody but me, anyway. So I saw what they didn't, Jenna's old boyfriend striding toward them with Z trailing inconspicuously.

He didn't give so much as a shout of warning. One second, Brett was moving his hand slowly up Jenna's shirt, and the next, he was sprawled on the floor, roaring in pain while his attacker continued the assault with low, brutal kicks.

Addie let loose with an ear-splitting shriek, and all across the club, conversations stopped.

It didn't take long for the other Blue Devils to overcome their surprise and enter the fray on their friend's behalf. The meathead was quickly dogpiled and subdued under a flood of athletes. But the fuse was lit, and there was no snuffing it now. If Z wants a fight—especially a big brawl in a crowded location—to continue, it's gonna continue.

"Get off him!" yelled a man who, as far as I could tell, was completely unrelated to anyone currently involved. He swung one of the space-age stools into the mass of athletes, and with a chorus of shouts, they let go of their original opponent.

Out of the corner of my eye, I saw Z talking to another man near the edge of the fight, looking very serious. A few seconds later, the man took off his jacket, and entered the fray.

In mere seconds, the Kosmos Lounge had become an all-out battleground. The bouncer stood helplessly at the edge of the fight, trying to figure out the safest way to get the situation under control. I didn't expect he'd have much luck.

"Kira, Addie, stay with me," I said, though I knew I didn't need to tell them. "Don't engage unless someone tries to start something."

Through the crowd of onlookers, cellphones were coming out. While most were being used to videotape the brawl (which involved, at this point, at least thirty people), a few people were clearly calling the cops. The bartender, too, was speaking urgently into a phone. He ducked a thrown bottle, which impacted a stack of glasses. They shattered with a strangely beautiful crashing noise.

Above the clamor, I heard police sirens rapidly

rising in volume. This fight wouldn't last much longer. Not that it needed to—several Devils were nursing injuries, and Brett's nose was leaking blood onto the floor where he lay, eyes half-closed. His team doggedly held their positions above him, keeping him from further harm, but he certainly wouldn't be playing tomorrow.

I was glad to see people looking out for him. Even if he *did* remind me of a younger, more athletic Lucas, even if he *was* clearly some kind of extra-concentrated douchebag, I didn't want him to suffer permanent damage. Same with everyone else. I'd signed off on the plan knowing that people would get hurt, but I was still holding out hope—perhaps naively—that nobody'd come to serious harm.

Almost the moment I thought that, I heard a sickening crunch and a particularly loud yell. A young blond man stumbled back, his arm twisted to an abnormal degree. My breath caught as I saw his shirt darkening rapidly.

The man who'd attacked him swung again, hitting him in the side with a broken bottle. The younger man's body seemed to fold around the blow and then he was down. Helpless.

Of *course* I'd known serious injuries were a possibility. But seeing them happen right in front of me was different. Despite my resolve to let the fight play out without interfering, my conscience wouldn't let me stand by.

"Kira—" I began, but Z got there first.

He came out of nowhere, tackling the man with the bottle and sending them both sprawling on the ground. Z recovered first and brought his knee up into the man's stomach.

My own stomach was churning, but I couldn't look away. Z's pretty tough—his dad taught him some moves—but he's also a magnet for misfortune. And running headlong into the swirling chaos of a bar fight is dangerous even for the luckiest of people. I knew if I took my eyes off him for even a split second, he'd be on the ground when I looked back. But at the same time, watching wouldn't stop it from happening.

"Get him out of there," Addie said to Kira. I heard the worry in her voice and knew she was thinking along the same lines.

No response.

I wrenched my eyes away from the fight to see what was going on. Addie was frozen, staring blankly into the Kira-shaped patch of air where Kira was supposed to be . . . and *wasn't.*

A dozen different profanities flashed through my head.

Z and the bottle-wielding man had both risen. Z charged and the man pivoted, smashing the bottle against the back of Z's head.

Z dropped like a stone.

But his opponent didn't seem to want the fight to end there. He raised his foot above Z's head—I flinched—and stumbled back as a small shot glass shattered against his chest. He looked right at us.

Or, at Addie, whose right arm was still outstretched from the throw.

When I figured out where Kira was, I was gonna *kill* her.

He took three long strides toward us before taking a poorly-aimed side kick to the chest from a Blue Devil.

"Nice shot," I said, and Addie nodded once, acknowledging the compliment.

The door flew open and the sirens became oppressively loud as blue uniforms poured into the room. That by itself was enough to stop the majority of the fight—most people weren't crazy enough to keep fighting in full view of law enforcement. What few pockets of fighting remained were cowed into submission in short order.

The moment the fighting had stopped, we ran to Z's fallen body, ignoring an officer's protests. He wore a pained grimace, but his eyes were open.

"That hurt like a bitch," he croaked. "Y'all think I'm pretty dumb, huh?"

"Biggest idiot in the room," I said. "What the hell were you thinking?"

But he could tell I was glad he was alright.

The three of us sat there on the floor, smelling the blood and booze and vomit, and listening to the crackle of police-standard radios.

"Had to," said Z. "He was a friend of mine."

As if that justified anything.

"My head look alright?" he asked, prodding it gingerly.

"On the outside, but you should see a doctor," said Addie, still looking a little shell-shocked.

"Don't think I've got a choice," Z muttered as a blue-uniformed LVPD officer approached us.

"You alright there, son?" he asked. "Did any of you catch what happened?"

That's when I realized we wouldn't be allowed to leave until we'd given statements and been thoroughly questioned, but at that point, it was far too late to change the plan.

TEN

I HALF-NOTICED ADDIE PUSH PAST ME TO ENGAGE the cop before he could draw me into the conversation. Good thing too, because I needed all my cognitive power focused on the problem at hand—namely, that my plan had just burst apart at the seams.

We'd made it all the way to the last step—*slip away in the confusion, then meet at the bus stop two blocks down.* Now Z was hurt (who knew how bad?), Kira was *missing*, and we were all persons of interest, about as far from *slipping away* as you can get. Any chance of escape had vanished when the cops arrived.

No, earlier—when Z'd taken a bottle to the head. If we'd left then, we'd have made it, but that would've involved leaving him behind. Not that he wouldn't have deserved it for running into the melee like an idiot. But that's not how the CPC operates. We're a team, and we act like one.

Except when we don't. Except when someone's *job* is to watch our backs and then *isn't there* when you need her. There wasn't a good enough excuse in the world for Kira, wherever she was. I'd been sweeping the room for her since the fight stopped, but it was even more crowded than it'd been before it started, so I wasn't having much luck.

Even worse, I didn't know *when* she'd disappeared, only when I'd noticed. In fact, the last time I'd seen her had been before the fight started—after that, I'd assumed she was behind me, keeping an eye on things. She could've been gone *well* before the police arrived, and therefore wasn't even necessarily *in* the Lounge itself.

I dunno why she'd have left. But I dunno why she'd have disappeared either.

At the door, a knot of people were trying unsuccessfully to push past the cops. We were stuck for now—if she'd been inside when the cops arrived, she was still here. Somewhere.

A hand touched my shoulder lightly. "He's gone," said Addie in my ear.

"What did you tell him?"

"Nothing. I said we had no idea what happened, that everything went crazy around us. He said to sit tight and wait for the ambulance."

"We ain't doing that, right?" Z sat up indignantly. "I've gotta do all kinds of shit tonight."

Addie and I looked at each other.

"You have a head injury," said Addie. "That's a pretty big deal."

"I feel great. Well," Z winced. "I feel good. Maybe just okay."

But he was blinking rapidly, and there was a dullness to his expression that worried me.

"We'll bring your laptop by the hospital," I said. "You can do the rest from there. Addie's right."

"And explain to my folks why their insurance is charging them for an ER visit in Vegas? They were already on the fence about letting me come."

"You could pay out of pocket," Addie suggested.

"You seen how much hospitals charge these days? Shit's expensive."

"I will *pay for it.*"

"I'm *fine*," snapped Z with uncharacteristic vehemence. Far from getting Addie to back off, though, this only caused a response in kind, and the Great Argument (interrupted briefly when a uniformed adult got too close) began. And what a sight to behold. Addie's a master of talking people into things, but Z had unparalleled social experience on his side, and he spotted every little guilt trip, every attempt to shift the focus back on him, every dirty trick in the book. When I realized, after ten long minutes of heated rhetoric, that neither party was gonna concede, I suggested we drop the argument and focus on getting out of here.

Addie's glare was less *et tu, Brutus?* than *what the fuck are you thinking, Brutus?*, but I gave her a little smile of solidarity when Z wasn't looking, and she calmed down enough for us to talk through a plan.

Getting Z out was the easy part. The EMTs, who'd arrived partway through the argument, were wheeling the wounded out on carts. One had stopped by to check up on us already and assured us that Z'd be tended to once the more seriously injured had been helped (Z'd somehow managed to hold in his protestations until they were out of hearing range). Of course, then he'd be in the medics' hands, which wasn't much better, but at least he'd be out of the bar—farther than the rest of us could get at this point.

Addie assured me she could get past the cops (I couldn't figure out how she'd do it, but I guess if I *could*, I could just sneak out myself). From there, she could lift some scrubs, pose as an EMT, and let Z out of the ambulance once nobody was looking. So that was two of us free.

Only it made sense for me to stay behind so we didn't all leave Kira in the lurch (even if that's exactly what I *wanted* to do). Addie and Z could handle the remainder of the job between them, and the cops would let everyone go *eventually*. Addie didn't bother hiding her relief when I suggested this—smuggling me out wouldn't have been easy.

At this point, Z's turn to receive medical attention couldn't be far away, so the sooner Addie got into position the better. "See you on the other side," I said, and she winked back.

Just before she vanished into the crowd, I sent her a text: Don't get him out.

She read it, turned around, and winked again.

With Addie's departure, the conversation lapsed into an uneasy quiet. Z seemed to have used most of his energy arguing with Addie, and was now the most taciturn I'd seen him in ages. It was almost a relief when the EMTs loaded him onto a stretcher and carted him out the door.

Addie and Z would do *their* part—it was up to me to find Kira. I cast another futile look around the crowded room. She could be *anywhere*—she wasn't even necessarily in the Kosmos Lounge. This could take all night—

"'Sup, bitch?"

—or all of five seconds.

I whirled around at the sound of Kira's voice. There she stood, calm and confident as ever. If she'd been dragged into the bar fight, it didn't show—she wasn't even sweating. And from her easy smile, I gathered that she wasn't expecting me to be angry.

"Where the fuck have you been?" I demanded.

Kira shrugged. "Around."

I folded my arms. That shit was *not* gonna fly.

"Checking on shit."

"You *do* know Z's hurt." My voice came out

flatter than I'd intended, like a dull knife. It was that or start shouting.

Kira's eyes flicked briefly towards the ground. "Again? That sucks."

"Sucks that you *weren't there to help him*!" I snapped with sudden fire.

"Like I said, I was dealing with some shit." Kira waved a hand noncommittally toward the center of the room. "Over there."

The only thing keeping me from wrapping my hands around Kira's throat was the knowledge that she could—and would—rip my arms off and beat me to death with them. I'd have to settle for a tirade. But just as I was about to launch into the mother of all homilies, I remembered the cops—I had a feeling they wouldn't react too well if I started screaming my head off right next to them. So instead, I took deep breath after deep breath and thought calming thoughts.

"*Shit*, this place is a mess," Kira said, trying heroically to fill the awkward pause as I focused on breathing. "We sure wrecked—*they*, I mean. Whoa, check that out!"

I didn't particularly want to look where she was pointing, but my curiosity got the better of me. Across the bar, currently being questioned, was the guy we'd spotted at Treasure Island Casino, the one who looked like the popsicle vendor.

"It's popsicle dude again!" said Kira. "You think he knows he's too old to party?"

Part of me wanted to dwell on the odds of seeing this guy both here *and* at Treasure Island, but I shook the urge away. Not important right now.

"Stop trying to distract me. You had one job—if someone's about to beat our asses, beat their ass first, twice as hard. So how did Z get his ass beat?"

I fixed her with a hard stare, and to my surprise, she squirmed away. Her pale cheeks were flushed with equal parts anger and embarrassment . . . and while the anger was no surprise, I could count the number of times Kira'd been *embarrassed* on one hand.

"You can start by promising it won't happen again," I prompted.

Kira's face tightened.

"The sooner you do, the sooner we can move on."

Finally, the words came, but begrudgingly, as if they were being dragged out of her throat by a tractor. "I won't fuck up again."

"Glad to hear it."

In as few words as possible, I outlined the situation, and for once, Kira actually stayed quiet long enough for me to finish.

" . . . and since getting us out might be tough, Addie and Z'll finish the job while we let the cops question us."

Kira's face screwed up in an expression I couldn't place at first, but then recognized as deep thought. "Why not just get out the same way *they* did?"

"Because I'm not—*oh.*"

I dunno what was worse—that I hadn't seen

it the moment Kira'd prompted me, or that I'd *needed Kira to prompt me.*

"That's a really good idea," I said, with the same reluctance she'd just apologized with, and she beamed.

It didn't take long for the EMTs to notice me once I lay supine and started moaning softly. My fingers were clamped firmly over my ribs, where the edges of a blood-soaked patch were barely visible (Kira'd suggested actually cutting me open, and I'm still not sure if she'd been joking).

"My boyfriend's hurt!" Kira was shrieking, and I did my best to sell it, keeping my face a pained grimace and lolling as best I could. "He's dying over here!"

Dying? I'd barely been able to wipe enough blood off the floor to imitate *hurt*—I couldn't sell *dying*. I wasn't even sure how that'd *look*.

Addie would've. She would've painted her face pale and stopped her heartbeat temporarily somehow. Alas, we can't all be future Oscar winners.

They loaded me onto a gurney. I moaned a little louder as they moved me, and kept my hand over my ribs to keep anyone from taking a closer look. As we wheeled towards the door, Kira kept pace with us, wailing about her dying boyfriend. But when we approached the door, a cop moved into her way. I flopped my head around a little so I could watch.

"Sorry, ma'am," he said. "We have to ask that you remain here."

"That's my *boyfriend*," said Kira, letting some edge into her tone.

"He'll be in good hands," said the cop. He was young and slight, with hair so dark it was almost blue. The EMTs ignored the conversation and kept moving. I was halfway through the door, and Kira's impassioned pleas didn't seem to be doing much. Then I was outside and I couldn't see them anymore. But I could hear them.

"Outta my way!"

This was followed by a shout of surprise, and then

Kira burst through the entrance and straight-up tackled the stretcher, heaving big fake sobs. I lifted my left arm weakly and patted her shoulder, trying not to lose my temper again. What part of *not attracting attention* had she misunderstood?

But I guess they decided pursuit was more trouble than it was worth, because nobody followed her out the door. It was left to the EMTs to talk her off of me—and slowly, painstakingly, they did, with Kira sniffling every second of the way.

This too was part of the plan. Once Kira and I were separated, the EMTs lost interest in her, leaving her free to text Addie so she could come get me, just like Addie had been supposed to do for Z.

There were four ambulances parked outside the Kosmos Lounge, surrounded by a milling crowd of white coats and stretchers. Whatever medical personnel they'd brought, it wasn't nearly enough. Fine with me—the more understaffed they were, the easier it'd be for Addie to slip past them unchallenged.

They wheeled me to the second closest ambulance, opened the big back door, and slid me inside. To my surprise, the space inside was already occupied by another stretcher, which was itself occupied. But that surprise was nothing to what I felt when I recognized its occupant.

"Yo," said Z.

"Uh . . . hey."

Was there a way for Addie to get me out and leave Z behind in a way he wouldn't notice? Preliminary thoughts indicated *no.* It was either go to the hospital with him or let him escape with me—or cause a scene leaving him behind.

No good options there.

I could've found my phone and warned Addie away. Then Z'd get the medical attention he needed.

But I didn't.

ELEVEN

ADDIE WASN'T HAPPY THAT Z'D AVOIDED THE hospital, but she at least had the sense not to flip out about it in his presence. She instead took her anger out on Kira for letting him get hurt in the first place. As you can imagine, Kira didn't take this too well.

While they yelled in the background, Z walked me through what he'd been doing while we were blackmailing Isaiah Porter. He'd been hanging around the underground, where the betting pools were largest and most popular. Even the Mafia was getting in on the action. I didn't believe him at first—were college sports that big of a deal? Z assured me they were.

"I wouldn't lie to my friends," he said. "But they introduced me to *their* friends, and, well, they're once removed at that point, right?"

I'd always known that Z would somehow justify doing his duty. He was a smart guy—he *had* to know that even if he wasn't misleading his friends in person, the rumor he'd helped start could leak back around to them anyway. But the brain's good at ignoring things like that. As far as Z's conscience went, he'd done enough to feel good about it, and that was what mattered. You could count on guys like him, no matter how much they whined beforehand.

The game's rigged in Duke's favor. Under Z's masterful tending, the rumor'd taken root in the intrigue-rich soil of the underworld. Now, so many people were betting on Duke that the bookies were adjusting their odds accordingly. A bet on a ten-point differential in favor of Maryland was hovering in the ballpark of six-to-one odds.

Before Z could say more, Addie dragged us into the argument, which raged for the better part of two hours before we agreed to call it quits. Kira was happy to admit she'd fucked up, but what she *wouldn't* do—and what Addie kept pressing her on—was explain *why*. Z was mad too, but shy about it, unwilling to make a big deal. I remembered what Addie'd said about him liking Kira . . . but he was probably just scared of her.

By the time we got to sleep, it was three-thirty. Or, as Kira called it, "My normal bedtime." Addie and Kira were still smoldering too much to sleep in the same bed, so Addie took the couch. I couldn't help but feel jealous that Kira got a bed to herself as I crawled under the covers next to an already-snoring Z

"Your snoring kept me awake all night," I informed him in the morning, and he hit me in the face with his pillow. But it hadn't been his snoring, not really—it'd been the sparks in the air, the electric thrill right before the end of a job. We'd thrown the ball, and now it'd either go through the net or it wouldn't—to use a topical metaphor. We could only watch and hope.

How could I sleep in the face of that kind of excitement?

By noon, we'd all managed to crawl out of bed.

"There's a couple articles about last night," said Kira, already behind the computer screen. She'd stretched out on the bed with the computer balanced on her chest and looked like she was about to fall asleep again at any second. "One mentions Brett in passing, but there's nothing else about basketball. Def no headlines like CONSPIRACY TO RIG NCAA STARTS FIGHT, HARMS PLAYERS."

"That's good." I said. "Would've been embarrassing if we'd accidentally drawn media attention to our own caper."

The risk had been there, and while I'd taken steps to mitigate it—like making sure the fight was large enough to draw attention away from the important participants—there was no getting rid of it entirely. I'd deemed it small enough to be worth the chance, and apparently I'd been right. As always.

"I've got one," said Addie. "FIGHT AT KOSMOS LOUNGE INJURES MANY, BLOCKHEAD REFUSES MEDICAL TREATMENT."

Z threw a cloth rag at her head. "I feel better now than you do on a *good* day."

"Are we in any pictures?" I asked, trying to defuse the situation. It was important to keep things professional, no matter how hard everyone else worked against me.

"Not so far," said Kira. "A bunch of people got video, but nobody's gonna watch them. We're probably good as long as we're not in the articles."

"Well, we know *you* wouldn't be in the pictures because you weren't fucking there when we needed you," Z groused.

Everyone stopped talking and looked at Kira. The room was suddenly thick with tension again. With good reason, because *come on*, she'd let us down hard, and didn't even have a good excuse. But Z was still a fucking idiot for bringing it up again.

"I told you I was busy with some other bullshit,"

said Kira. "Didn't expect you to rush in like a dumbass. Besides, how did someone even attack you? Doesn't everyone like you too much? You always—"

"Guys," I said quietly. "Let's not turn this into last night, okay? Kira knows she fucked up and said she'd watch our backs next time, so let's drop it for now. We've got a job to finish."

Z still didn't look satisfied, but he mumbled his assent from across the room.

"Great. Now, game's at six, so let's grab lunch, kill a couple hours, then watch our hard work pay off."

We'd talked about actually going to the game, but I'd decided it made more sense to watch from the comfort of our hotel room. We wouldn't be able to influence events on-scene at the last minute if things went horribly wrong, but there was no chance of being confronted by Isaiah Porter or recognized by Brett's teammates either. And if something *did* go wrong, what could we do, run out onto the court?

(*No* is the answer I'm looking for).

By T-minus-thirty, the resentment had faded from everyone's expressions, though a little occasionally snuck into our (well, *their*) voices. But we could laugh with each other and swallow our bitter remarks. We were headed into the endgame as a team—the way things were *supposed* to be.

At T-minus-ten, Z turned on the TV and switched over to Fox Sports, where reporters were leading up to the game with an overview of the teams.

"*. . . Duke, originally favored to win, lost three of its star players to recent injuries, which has put something of a damper on their morale,*" said a sports commentator, identified by some floating text as Danielle Kirkpatrick. "*Preliminary investigation has found no evidence of foul play by the University of Maryland, so, bad luck for the Devils! Duke fans have suggested delaying the game, but no official request has been made.*"

"Well, that's that, then," I said, but we were too focused on the upcoming game to care. It was hard to be excited about getting away with it when we didn't know if we'd actually succeeded yet.

Danielle Kirkpatrick proceeded to summarize the state of the league (Down to the famous "Final Four," with this match's winner going on to play against either Berkeley or Chicago), the various deeds of star players on both teams (Brett Tarquin had scored thirty-two points against Memphis earlier this season), and the intensity of the rivalry between Duke and Maryland (which had me almost believing, after a few minutes, that we'd been hired by a Maryland alum). And then the game was starting. T-minus-zero.

"Here we go, bitches," said Kira. She was gripping the table so hard in excitement that her knuckles were turning white.

The jump ball at the beginning went to Maryland, as predicted by Danielle Kirkpatrick before the game (Brett had been Duke's designated jumper). That served as an accurate metaphor for the general flow of the game after that. Within the first five minutes, Maryland was maintaining a tenuous but tangible six-point lead, aided and abetted by referee Porter, who'd clearly taken our little talk to heart.

"*Thweeeet!*" went the whistle, indicating a foul as Duke attempted to drive through Maryland's defense. A scowling Don Kzowszki, who'd taken Brett's position as power forward, was again forced to forfeit control of the ball. There were loud boos from the crowd, who'd figured out that fairness was not among Isaiah's current priorities. Thankfully, he soon remembered he was supposed to present a slightly more neutral facade and started diversifying his calls. At that point, though, the damage was done. Duke's already-low morale had only plunged and they were now down nine points after a wonderful three-point shot from Maryland center player Norman Dilling—just one away from the ten-point spread we needed.

Duke called time out soon after.

"I don't wanna jinx it, but good job, guys," said Z, firing off air-fives around the room.

Addie was less sure. "We aren't even halfway through yet. Don't start celebrating."

Duke was burning with new fire when they retook the court. Whatever the coach had said, it must've been legendary—an eleventh-hour speech right out of a sports movie. If I ever needed a motivational speech written, I knew who I'd ask.

And they were making a comeback. Maryland was only five points up now . . . then three. Every new basket inspired them all over again. And in the absence of Brett Tarquin, the team had rallied behind Don Kzowszki. He'd taken some knocks last night, but a doctor hadn't explicitly ordered him off the court, so he'd elected to play—and he was playing twice as hard in his fallen teammates' honor.

"And that's the half!" said Danielle Kirkpatrick brightly. *"Looks like Duke's still in the game after all. We'll be back after halftime."*

And with that, a saccharine-sweet shampoo commercial took over where she'd left off—much to Z's delight.

"There's no way they can actually bring this back, right?" I asked.

Kira laughed. "No way. They'll go back to folding any time now. Duke hasn't been up all game."

"So it can't possibly happen later," said Addie sarcastically, flopping back on the couch. "It's anyone's game at this point."

"Point of order," said Z. "I'm pretty sure I'm the only one here who's ever watched basketball before today."

"I saw a game once," said Kira slowly. "By accident."

Z folded his arms and turned back to the TV, where a disembodied female voice was promising that this shampoo would make my hair shine like polished gold.

"Well? Any insights to offer, O Basketball Master?" Addie was unwilling to let the matter drop.

"It'll be Maryland, I'm pretty sure" said Z. "That's my gut. Don can't keep playing, they'll sub him out soon. After that, it's up to the rest to keep momentum going. Can they do it? Who knows?"

"Let's not forget Isaiah," I pointed out.

The second half began much like the first had ended, with a rallying charge from Don Kzowszky through Maryland's defense that ended in another basket for Duke.

"C'mon!" yelled Z at the TV. "He was right there, guys!" He shook his head in disbelief.

Maryland took the ball up the court, but a mis-aimed pass was intercepted by—again—Don, and taken right down the center.

"Fucking shitbag cocks!" That one was Kira.

Don neared the basket, lined up his shot . . . and his leg gave out beneath him, sending him sprawling. Isaiah blasted his whistle, but play was already stopped and Duke's coach was running to the side of his team's last hope.

The decision took a few minutes, but there was only one possible outcome. Don limped off the court to applause from both camps—respectful from Duke supporters, grateful from Maryland.

"*. . . Mr. Kzowszky suffered an injured leg in the same incident that left three teammates on the sidelines. When given the option to play or sit out, Kzowszky chose to play—and gave quite a showing, considering his injuries. But it looks like that leg caught up with him.*"

The loss of a fourth player had Duke scrambling to keep their momentum up, a task which quickly proved impossible in the face of a revitalized Maryland, which was pressing its numerical advantage by switching out their tired players with a regularity Duke couldn't match. Combined with a pair of questionable calls from the referee in our corner, Maryland soon regained its lead, and reached the magic ten-point spread with six minutes to spare. Duke responded by calling another time out.

They returned energized, but without the wind that'd accompanied their first return—after all, one could hardly expect Duke's coach to have a *second* rallying speech in his back pocket. Nobody outside of a Hollywood movie is *that* good.

By the time the buzzer went off, Maryland was eighteen points up.

The stadium exploded with cheers, as if to pretend they hadn't seen this coming for ten minutes now.

I spread my arms wide. "Congratulations, friends, on another job well done."

The lack of suspense was, on the one hand, disappointing, but that was the price of a well-planned job. I'd take a dozen boring jobs over a single failure any day. And this was never gonna be complex compared to, say, rigging a poker game. It was whatever was coming *next* that was exciting.

I couldn't wait to discover what it was.

And if you have an emotional attachment to Duke . . . no hard feelings, right?

TWELVE

"YOU KNOW, THE JOB AIN'T OVER YET," SAID Z. We stopped, confused, and he stared solemnly back. And then . . .

"Don't tell me y'all forgot the part where we party it the fuck up!" he whooped, discarding his poker face in favor of a wide, face-splitting smile.

"Hell yeah!" shouted Kira.

"A very astute point," I said, allowing a smile of my own. "I'm ashamed to say I forgot that step, thus placing the entire job in jeopardy. But I promise, it's not too late to salvage it."

"That's the spirit," said Z. He stood. "Ladies and gentlefolk—and Jason—I humbly request permission to take over for our esteemed planner, given his shortcomings in planning the celebration for such an occasion as our success."

"Nice work," said Kira. "You sounded like Addie for a minute there. Now go back to normal, Addie-Z is weird."

Z looked to the rest of us for backup, but we nodded our agreement.

"Fine," he said. "How about . . . Guys, can I take over party planning since Jason fucked up?"

"Much better."

I still wasn't convinced planning the celebration was my area of responsibility, since it wasn't technically part of the job itself. But I was hardly gonna give up that power now that it'd landed on my lap. At least, not without making a show of it.

"How *dare* you attempt to usurp me," I said haughtily, shooting a severe look at Z.

"Nah," said Kira. "I'm with Z. Your parties are shit."

I looked at Addie, but she shook her head, her green eyes sparkling with mischief. "I think it's time you relinquished power to someone who knows how to use it."

"I guess I'm outvoted," I said. "Very well, Z, you have your wish. I suppose you have something ready to go?"

Z grinned. "Something like that. Heard a tip from a friend. Past that, I'll keep it a surprise."

Z's "surprise" was a small pizza parlor several blocks off the Strip. Despite its run-down appearance—the dark streaks running down the brick looked like old blood from at least three separate murders—the burnt-out sign still bravely advertised itself as *Brickhearth Pizza, High Quality Italian Cuisine.* We walked in mainly because we didn't want to hurt Z's feelings.

Brickhearth Pizza's interior was less sketchy than its exterior, but only just. The tables were wood, the chairs were red plastic, and the floor pattern would be best described as "stain-chic." To my great surprise, there were several customers, all wearing identical regretful expressions as they picked at their food.

Z, to his credit, seemed undeterred.

"I change my vote," said Kira.

"Too late," said Z, stepping up to the counter. "Hello, there."

"What are you looking for today," said the cashier, with all the monotone the lack of a question mark implies.

"How to get the fuck outta here," Kira whispered.

"Well, I'm not really feeling the menu," said Z, gesturing to the wall behind the counter where the (limited) menu was advertised. "I was hoping for something a little more south of the border, you get me?"

The cashier's demeanor didn't *change*, exactly, but there was a flicker of acknowledgement. "Right this way, please."

"C'mon," said Z. Behind the counter was a large and official-looking set of double doors, which he opened like he owned the place. We exchanged apprehensive looks and followed.

"Over/under on Z being the secret mastermind

behind everything that's ever happened to us, and here's where he reveals his twisted plan?" Addie muttered to me.

"I'll lowball. Thirty percent. Fifty if his plan was just to fuck with us."

Walking through the doors put us practically in the kitchens, but Z turned ninety degrees and pulled open a small door that was almost the same color as the surrounding wall. I could make out stairs leading down.

"Déjà vu," I said to Addie. "Hey Z, there a poker game down there?"

"Only one way to find out," said Z, beginning the descent.

I followed. The stairs were dimly lit by a flickering fluorescent light and smelled faintly of mildew. At the bottom was another door just as small as the one we'd come through. Taped onto it was a paper with the words *STORAGE BASSMENT* scrawled on it.

Now, it was either my superior intellect or that

I've had experience with secret basement areas, but I very much doubted that a storage basement (or "bassment," whatever that was) lay beyond that door.

And lo, I was right. I emerged into a room just as large as the main restaurant area above—and about ten times fancier.

"Whoa," said Kira, who'd been behind me. "Restaurantception."

The room was softly and tastefully lit by a large chandelier in the center, around which several marble tables were arranged. Two were occupied by serious-looking people in dress clothing, but the other three were available. A short, Hispanic gentleman dressed all in white sat in a solitary chair nearby, but stood as we entered.

"Good evening, sirs and madams," he said with a small bow. "Party of four? Right this way."

He gave us a table by the far wall, which was decorated with hanging tapestries. Then he passed us our menus, bowed politely again (reminding me of Jeeves) and made a graceful exit.

"Z," I said, looking at the menu with confusion. "This is a Mexican restaurant."

Z nodded rapidly. He looked far too pleased with himself.

"Can you explain why there's a high-end Mexican restaurant under the crappy pizza place upstairs?"

Z's rapid nodding changed to rapid shaking.

"Let me guess," said Addie "Friend of yours tipped you off?"

Back to nodding.

"I dunno about you," said Kira, "but I'm hungry as hell, so I'm just gonna go with it."

Addie and I stared at Z.

The place was just too *weird* to believe that Z'd just heard about it from a friend—hell, *I* wasn't sure it existed and I was standing in it. Sure, there was probably some wacky story about how they'd discovered it, and then let Z in on the secret during an amusing anecdote-swap, but it could also be (and probably was) a criminal venue.

If there's one thing I know, it's that the criminals with a sense of humor are the scariest ones. You'd think that given the popularity of *Batman*, this would be more widespread knowledge, but it's not exactly intuitive.

"The food's supposed to be great," said Z. "I remembered you guys are okay with Mexican, and I figured hey, when are we gonna get another opportunity to visit a place like this?"

I put my misgivings aside for now. Z didn't look worried, and he was kinda the expert on this place. Besides, I was hungry. "Well, Kira's happy, and you're happy, so I guess I'm happy."

Our waiter soon returned with water and complimentary chips, then took our orders. As you'll remember, I can't stand menus, but I finally decided on the tamale platter and the salsa sampler with a side of rice—and a Mexican Coke, because those aren't always easy to find. The waiter retreated once more with his hands full of menus, leaving a quiet filled only by the lilting salsa music in the background.

Addie broke the silence first. "I don't know about the rest of you, but I can't think of a better way to have spent my spring break."

"Hear, hear," echoed Kira.

"I know we technically dissolved the Club for Perfect Cleanliness," continued Addie, "but given recent events, I think we should continue working together. We're too good a team to stay split."

I couldn't keep the smile off my face. I'd been hoping for—and betting on—this result, but to have it officially suggested, and by *Addie* of all people, was the cherry on the job-well-done sundae.

"I'm down," said Z. "So long as Jason's really reformed, mind. Maybe one day, I won't be the one who gets screwed over.

"Maybe when Hell freezes over," I said. "Guys, you know my thoughts on this. I'm ready to reinstate the dream team whenever you are."

We all looked at Kira.

"Well, if you guys are doing it!" she said with a knife-edged grin. "I mean, I know how much you need me."

"I need you like I need an audit from the IRS," I said.

Addie froze. "Don't even joke about that."

"I wasn't finished!" said Kira. "I'm in, on one condition. We have to upgrade the name to reflect our new, improved nature."

I let out a loud, fake gasp. "You mean . . . the Club for *Double*-perfect Cleanliness?"

"The Z-team," suggested Z. He'd suggested that exact name at our first meeting, too.

Kira shoved him. "Stop trying to make it happen, bruh. It sucks."

"The Z-unit," he tried. "Actually, I kinda like that one."

"Dude, no."

"Z for Zendetta."

" . . . That one didn't even make sense."

"Yeah, you're done," Addie agreed. "My turn.

What about just "the team"? Then we could use it in public and nobody would catch on . . . "

"Too boring," said Kira immediately.

Addie and Z simultaneously began laying into Kira for shooting down ideas without contributing any, but before they could straighten out which of them should talk first, the food arrived.

"Shit, that was fast," said Z, immediately forgetting the argument and tucking in. I followed suit, trying my best to forget that I was technically in the basement of a pizzeria. It really *was* good.

I wasn't quite finished when my smartphone buzzed. A new e-mail, no subject.

Congratulations on a job well done. The second installment of your payment is on its way.

It was unsigned.

"Hey Kira, can you get anything out of this address?" I said, sliding the phone over to her.

"No prob," she said. She opened her laptop bag and pulled out her computer. "Someone get the Wi-Fi password."

Z looked at Addie. Addie and I looked at Z.

"Fine," he sighed.

"I got the e-mail too," said Addie, now also looking at her phone. "We all probably did."

"Seems kind of anticlimactic," I said. "Aren't we supposed to be inducted into their secret society now? Instead, we're just getting paid and sent on our way? I feel so *used.*"

"Get used to it," said Addie. "Such is our lot in life."

"It's 'n-o-l-e-d-i-j-e-s'," said Z, returning. "No caps or spaces."

"That's ominous," said Addie to nobody in particular.

Kira's hands moved over the keyboard at their normal frenetic pace. Her food sat abandoned beside the laptop as she worked.

"Now that we know we're getting paid, it's time for the traditional question," I said. "What's everyone doing with their cut?"

"Probably getting a car," said Z slowly. "I'm

like, *this* close to getting my license, and my bud at the Porsche dealership downtown can maybe get me a discount. Maybe I'll mod it, I dunno."

Kira didn't answer, like she hadn't heard the question. Maybe she hadn't—she sometimes went into a trance-like state when she was concentrating.

"Kira's gonna start *The Kira Show* for real," I said. "Addie?"

"Oh, I don't know," she said with a devious smile. "I was thinking I'd take you out to dinner."

"Ha, ha."

"Are you turning me down?" she pressed.

"I—no, but—you're serious?" Z was laughing silently behind her, and I resolved to get my revenge later. Even a superior intellect like mine can get caught off guard. So there.

"Am I in the habit of joking around? Look, if you're going to say no—"

"No. I mean, no, I'm not. I mean, yes . . . Can I start over?"

There was something disarming about that

small-mouthed smile in conjunction with Z's voiceless laughter in the background.

"Take your time," she said, sounding pleased.

I took a deep breath and prepared myself. "I would be honored to accept your invitation." As soon as I said it, I realized how clunky it sounded.

Addie's smile grew wider. "Good."

Behind her, Z began a slow clap.

"Oh, shut up," she said. "Or I'll tell Kira you—"

"What?" said Kira, peeking her head over the laptop. Slowly, her gaze passed over us. "Jace looks like he just got laid. Did I miss something?"

I rearranged my expression at once and added Kira to the "revenge" list.

"Nope," said Addie. "Find anything?"

"It's a throwaway address. Can't tie it to anything."

"Oh, fuck," said Z loudly.

Around the restaurant, heads turned towards us. Z stared blankly at them until they went back to their meals.

"I kinda expected that," said Kira. "The last one was the same. Why're you freaking out?"

"Not that," said Z. "I just got this text."

Kira took the phone first. Her mouth tightened. Then, without a word, she handed it to me.

ya crazy!!! did u hear the mob rigged it tho?

I passed it to Addie.

"If you're looking for context, that's the latest in a chain about the recent Duke/Maryland game," said Z quietly. "My friend is reliable."

He let the implication sink in.

"The mob hired us?" said Addie. "That makes little to no sense."

"This is bad," said Z. "The Mafia doesn't like loose ends."

"Well, the job's over," said Kira. "Let's just take our pay and go home. It's not like we pissed them off."

"Kira, if they're planning on actually paying us and *not* tying things up by slitting our throats and cementing us into Hoover Dam, I'll eat my bike. I'll send you a recording."

I flicked my eyes towards the exit, half-expecting a gang of slick-looking mobsters to pour out the small door and start shooting. But Addie was right—this made no sense. Why would the Mafia hire four teenagers and then kill them? Hiring us made sense, if they wanted to test our skills in an uncontrolled environment. So did killing us, if we'd ripped one of them off in the poker game. But doing both was just . . . *dumb.*

Lucas was in my head again. *Never underestimate human stupidity, Jason. Don't think that because* you *are too smart to take an action that your opponents will be.*

I'd been hearing *that* one since I could understand human speech—it was one of his favorites. But as much as I hated his sociopathic aphorisms bouncing around in my skull, I had to admit he had a point this time.

"Okay," I said. "Addie, you're right, it doesn't

make any sense. But if *Z*'s right, the consequences of ignoring him are kinda fatal. So with that in mind, we're gonna pack our things, buy new tickets, and skip town. If they wanna pay us, they can wire it. If they wanna offer us positions in their organization, there's video chat."

"Thank you!" exploded Z. "Finally!"

There were murmurs of assent from Kira and Addie as they realized the undeniable logic of my argument.

"I'll pay," said Z, hopping up. "Don't worry about it."

Z, offering to pay? He really *was* spooked.

In short order, we'd paid and all but run up the stairs and out of Brickhearth Pizza. The Strip was a short hike away, but once we were there, it took mere seconds to flag down a taxi. They were *everywhere.*

"Assuming the mob *did* hire us, and *does* want us dead, how exactly does flying back to New York, aka Mob Central, help us?" asked Addie suddenly.

"Shit," said Z. "I hadn't thought of that."

"I'll think of something," I said. "I have the whole plane ride to figure it out."

Plans where you have multiple consecutive hours to think have the best chance of going well. It's those times that you're suddenly thrust into a new situation that you sometimes miss important details. Which is unfortunate, since even one missed detail can throw everything into jeopardy.

"Remember, odds are we're overreacting," said Addie. "We should really try to straighten this out first."

"Yes," said Z caustically. "Just send the guy a reply. 'Excuse me, sir, but are you planning to have us killed? Please be honest.'"

The taxi pulled up to the Hilton, just as the shuttle had when I'd first arrived.

And I still hadn't realized.

We paused the conversation briefly to pay the cabbie, and then again as we passed through the hotel lobby, but it continued the moment we entered the elevator.

"Addie, buy the tickets," I said. "Sorry, but you're the least unpacked."

"Fair enough," she said.

The numbers ticked up slowly, one by one, as we approached our floor.

And I still hadn't realized.

We were out of the elevator before the doors finished opening. We went left, right, right again, and there was Room 843. Addie reached for the knob.

And *that's* when I realized.

"Shit," I swore. "They bought this room for us. They *know where we're staying.*"

But I was a few seconds too late. Addie'd already opened the door.

Even one missed detail . . .

Two men stood inside. Big men with swarthy complexions, dark hair, and identical small handguns pointed right at our chests.

"INSIDE," SAID THE TALLER ONE, MOTIONING WITH his gun.

We complied. Don't give me shit for it—you wouldn't have done differently. The shorter man closed the door behind us.

Z shrugged. "Saw it coming," he said to Addie. Addie's mouth twitched upward slightly.

"Our car is in the garage," said the man who'd spoken before, ignoring Z. "We will escort you to the elevator. You will press the button B-four."

"Before what?"

Tall looked confused. "No, the button—oh. Funny man."

I sighed. "Not a fan of comedy, I take it."

Kira's eyes were darting about the hallway, looking for potential weapons, but the men had preempted her—the hallway's previous contents were piled behind them.

"If you run or shout, we shoot," said Tall. "This, we do not want to do, since shots are loud. We do not like attention. But if you leave us no choice, we will shoot and brave the consequences. You understand?"

"I think *I* do," said Kira.

"Pretty straightforward, honestly," said Addie. "Easy to follow. Good job."

Tall grimaced like he'd swallowed curdled milk and I felt a small surge of pride for my friends, who never fail to deliver at being annoying. Most of the time, I curse them for it, but it occasionally proves its worth.

"Before we go, can you clarify some things? Like, why you hired us for such an easy job if you were just gonna kill us afterwards?"

Might as well try and put the puzzle together in case it helped me find a way out of this mess.

Predictably, the two mobsters—or so I assumed due to the circumstances of their arrival as well as their Italian accents and appearance—ignored me. Instead, Short patted us down and relieved us of our phones and wallets. It occurred to me that Short hadn't yet said a word (also that Short was a misnomer, since both men were pretty big).

"Move," said Tall. After a few moments of hesitation, we reluctantly turned around and opened the door. We didn't encounter anyone as we walked back down the hallway, though it wouldn't have mattered—the guns were shielded from view, by us from the front and the mobsters themselves from the back.

"Express it," said Tall once we were in the elevator.

"Huh?"

"Press B-four and the close door button and hold them down until we start moving."

I did so, again because I couldn't see anything else to do.

Our lack of bullet wounds seemed obviously directly related to the proximity of bystanders, and our lives wouldn't be spared much longer after that obstacle stopped existing. That, at least, gave us some time. Time I could use to find a way out.

There was bribery and blackmail—there always was. But I had no blackmail on them, and as for bribery, the Mafia takes loyalty to their *famiglia* pretty seriously. So those were both probably out.

We (meaning Kira) could overcome them physically, but that relied on their giving her an opening. So far they'd conducted themselves professionally, so I couldn't count on them slipping up.

We could all run at once, but at least one of us would almost certainly die, even if we started running as soon as we rounded a corner. If the mobsters were carrying guns, they could probably aim them too.

Even if I *did* think of something, I'd have to

communicate it to the others without talking, somehow. Discussing escape plans would probably anger our captors. Besides, they'd hear everything we thought of.

When the elevator *ding*ed on the fourth basement level, I still had nothing. Which meant if I thought of something later that involved the elevator, I'd be shit out of luck. If the plan involved the *parking garage*, I'd need to think of it pretty much *now*.

Nothing came to mind.

At Tall's urging, we walked down half a ramp, turned the corner, and stopped in front of a silver Escalade SUV. Short got into the driver's seat while Tall sat in the back with us. The engine revved.

"In hindsight," I said, "I really should've—"

"No talking," said Tall, poking me with his gun.

"Save it for the amateurs. Talk can't help me now, and you won't shoot me for it as long as I'm just chatting. As I was saying . . . " Just as I'd predicted, Tall hadn't stepped in again, though he *was* looking at me like I was a piece of old gum he'd found stuck to his shoe. "In hindsight, I really should've moved us into a different hotel."

Lucas would've mocked that mistake *merci-lessly*—I know that because it's what my personal head-Lucas was doing. Now I *had* to find a way out, if only to spit in that old bastard's face.

"I usually don't miss that kind of thing," said Addie disgustedly. "If I hadn't been so surprised to see you . . . "

"I don't think it would've mattered. If it were me, I'd have had spies watching the room to let me know if they, *we*, moved."

"Too wasteful," said Z. "Why bother?"

"Why bother paying us and *then* killing us?" I said. "*That's* wasteful. They did it anyway." I turned around in my seat to look at Tall, who was watching the conversation tight-lipped. "C'mon. Tell us what the hell happened there. I won't tell anyone. Since I'm about to be shot and all."

My attempt at conversation yielded nothing, except being glowered at by a pair of narrow eyes.

It was bribery time. It wouldn't work, but I had to at least *try*. "Hey, we still have the advance you paid us. We could return it—we haven't spent it yet. We give you the money, you let us go—"

"Stop," said Tall in that rough, accented voice.

Oh, well. I hadn't expected any better. Addie patted me on the hand as if to say *good try*. I turned my hand palm-up, caught hers, and gave it a reassuring squeeze. She smiled at me, and the backseat of the Mafia-mobile suddenly didn't seem like such a bad place to be.

It was Tall, surprisingly, who broke the silence. "We didn't pay you any advance."

That was even *more* surprising.

"Um."

"Well, this is awkward," said Z. "Because I definitely got paid. You guys did too, right?"

"Would've raised a fucking riot if I hadn't," said

Kira. "So, uh . . . I guess I shouldn't be thanking you, huh."

This may not seem like much of a lifeline, but when you're drowning, *everything's* a lifeline.

"Hold, hold, hold, wait a moment," I said. "Mr. Mafioso, there's a major discrepancy here. Surely, stopping the car and straightening this out is far more important than carrying out your assigned task on schedule, like a drone. You're better than that. You're more professional than that."

There was no response from either of our potential killers. Again.

"Aren't you even a *bit* curious?"

"I know *I* am," said Addie. "Someone out there representing the Mafia paid us two hundred thousand dollars when he didn't need to. There's a Mafia account missing two hundred thousand dollars thanks to that man. And the only people who could help solve the case—and return the cash—are about to be executed for what I'm sure is a particularly shoddy reason. Not that I'd *know*, since none of us have any idea what that reason *is*, but I'd call it a pretty safe bet."

The vibration of the engine against my leg changed timbre and then stopped altogether. We'd pulled over.

"Out, Cloudface," said Short. "The rest of you, stay."

Tall—who apparently went by "Cloudface" with his Mafia buddies—scowled. "Are you sure?"

"*Sí, idiota!*" snapped Short. Z started, and I swear the car rattled a bit with the force of his exclamation. When Cloudface hesitated, Short opened his own door and got out. "I will be waiting," he said mockingly.

Cloudface reluctantly opened the door. "Stay here," he growled. "And don't think to try anything."

The first thing I did once the door closed behind him was check if Short had left the keys. He hadn't.

"Well shit," said Kira. "Ain't that a twist."

"If a clerical error saves us, I'll marry Jeeves," I said. "But stay alert and take an opportunity if you see it."

Addie gave me a scornful look, as if to say, *What do you think I am, an idiot?*

I looked out the window. We were in a suburban area outside downtown Las Vegas. Not murder territory. Yet. Cloudface and Short were arguing heatedly in Italian by the hood, but they could get back in and keep driving any minute.

"Shit," Z muttered to himself. "What was his name?"

I looked at him. He'd wedged himself into a corner and was staring blankly into space. I scooted over and put my arm around his shoulder.

"Z, dude, don't go crazy on me."

Z shrugged my arm off. "Stop it. I'm trying to think."

That, I could respect. I sank back onto the gray upholstery and rubbed my temples. The car was too warm, and sweat was pooling on my back. It was almost a relief when the opening door let a breeze in.

"False alarm," said Cloudface, climbing back in. "It was a good try, though."

Short climbed back into the driver's seat and revved up the engine.

"No more delays," said Cloudface, and Short nodded.

Short drove a couple hours more, far from the city lights. We tried to keep the banter flowing, but it became increasingly stale and forced until finally, it died altogether.

Finally, the car ground to a halt again. We'd long since left the markers of civilization behind us, and when I looked out the window, all I could see was a sea of black.

We were gonna die.

It hit me suddenly, in a way it hadn't before. I guess I'd been holding out hope that this was all a big joke, but seeing the pitch-black landscape outside the SUV drove the situation home. An icy chill settled over my skin.

"You sure we can't offer you anything?" asked Kira. Her voice sounded oddly scratchy and hoarse.

Cloudface opened the car door. "Nothing."

"Stay with the car," said Short. He opened his door too. "I will take them."

"Out," growled Cloudface.

Z was the first out. He didn't look too bad, all things considered. Somehow, his calmness affected me and I found myself breathing easier as I stepped into the night. Cloudface had to wrestle Kira out of the car, and I expected her at any moment to start fighting back, but Short was covering her with his handgun. Eventually, they got her out.

"Hey," said Z, putting a hand on her arm. "It'll be OK. Deep breaths."

He looked more concerned with Kira's distress than his own approaching fate, and in that moment, I believed Addie—Z had a crush, and he was doing his best to hide it. Poor guy. Not that I was any better.

"Walk," said Short. And we did, because we had no other choice.

We walked in silence over sand and rock. By some unspoken agreement, Addie and I were side by side. Our hands found each other in the dark, and we folded our fingers together. I wanted to say something to her, but my throat felt clogged, so I just looked behind me and watched as the car's headlights got dimmer and dimmer until I couldn't see them anymore.

And then Z cleared his throat.

"Tony," he softly, before the shattered silence had a chance to reassert itself. "Don't do this."

Short stopped abruptly, as if Z's words had caught him by the lapels. "What's that?"

"You don't recognize me," said Z. "I get it. I didn't recognize you either. Not until you spoke."

I felt a sudden, wild stab of hope.

"Sleepaway camp?" Z prompted. "I was seven. You were older."

"Twelve," said Tony. "Zethus? Is this some kind of joke?"

"No joke, my friend," said Z. "Just my shitty luck. What're you doing in Nevada?"

"What are *you* doing in Nevada?"

"Your guys flew me out and then tried to kill me."

"Right." Tony seemed to gather himself. "I'm sorry this is how we meet again. No hard feelings, Zethus? You must understand my loyalty to the *famiglia* comes above our friendship."

"I guess I figured that, yeah," said Z. "You're a very honorable guy, Tony."

"Yes," said Tony. "I am."

"I bet your word's everything to you."

No sound but the wind whistling across the flatland.

"Ah," said Z triumphantly. "You remember."

"I was a boy then," hissed Tony.

"But you gave your word."

Again, Tony made no reply. I wanted to burst out cheering, but I kept quiet. Noise might disrupt Z's mojo.

"One favor," said Z. His voice was low, but steady. "Anything I want. Tony, I'm calling it in. Let me and my friends go. By the oath you swore."

"But all you did was—"

"Hey, I didn't *ask* you to swear. That's on you for offering more than my favor was worth."

"*Cosa Nostra—*"

"Tell them you killed us," said Z. "We won't come back. We'll leave the criminal business. They won't know the difference. We're just kids, Tony!"

"You were a good friend," said Tony, raising his gun. "But I wish I'd never met you."

He fired.

I flinched backwards, then realized I wasn't dead. Neither, as a brief look confirmed, was anyone else.

Tony fired again, and this time I noticed how

his gun pointed out into the distance, nowhere close to hitting any of us.

Two more times he fired, and then he lowered his gun, and silence reigned once again in the Nevada desert.

I stood entirely motionless, in case moving would change his mind.

“Goodbye, Zethus,” said Tony at last. And then he turned around and walked back the way he’d come.

“Goodbye, Tony,” said Z to his retreating back. Tony gave no indication that he’d heard, but the night was so silent he could hardly have missed it.

Then he was gone, swallowed up by the sea of black. Several minutes later, we heard the revving of an engine.

And we were again alone in the darkness.

FOURTEEN

IT FELT LIKE FOREVER, WALKING BACK ALONG THAT road towards the City of Sin.

The sky was lightening as we reached the first small town. We sat outside a deserted gas station, tired and hungry, and waited until the morning attendant arrived.

He was surprised to find four teenagers sitting outside his door, and it took some convincing before he'd let us use his phone, but we were finally able to call a taxi. After that, I fell asleep. The next thing I remember is Addie shaking me awake in a Motel Six parking lot, and then—dimly—Kira pushing a door open. I *don't* remember crawling into bed, but I must've, because when I woke up, I was curled up under the covers with Z snoring next to me. Light was streaming in through the curtains, and the digital clock perched on the bedside table read three thirty-eight p.m.

I felt like shit.

Kira was sitting at the table, drumming softly with her fingers. I wondered idly if she'd slept, then staggered off to the bathroom and turned on the shower. Ten minutes later, I was starting to feel like a person again.

I opened the bathroom door ready to face the day and immediately noticed that Addie'd come back. There were two-and-a-half Subway sandwiches and some coffee cups sitting on the table by Kira, which explained where she'd been.

"Morning," she said. "Tuck in."

I hugged her instead. For a moment, we were two kids happy for each other's company. Then we released each other and it was all business.

"Alright, fill me in," I said, grabbing half a sandwich

and examining the room. It was a significant downgrade from the Hilton, but given the circumstances, I was perfectly happy with the tradeoff. "You gave the front desk a fake name, right?"

"Mmm-hmm."

"And the—"

"And the wrong number of people, yes," said Addie. "Just like you told us."

I blinked, confused. And the headache wasn't helping matters. I took a long sip of coffee, hoping it would help.

"You know, last night. In the parking lot."

"Don't remember," I said, and drank a little more coffee.

"You reeled off a whole bunch of instructions," said Kira from the table. "Some really twisty, paranoid shit. You seriously don't remember?"

I shrugged. Apparently, I was capable of thinking things through *on autopilot.* I've never been prouder of my subconscious.

"Well, we did it all anyway," said Kira. "Gave

the front desk all kinds of fake info, set it up so our shit from the hotel's being delivered—"

"Wait, being delivered *here*?"

"No," said Addie quickly. "To an entirely separate room, to be recovered once we've determined it's safe."

"And the person in charge of collecting it—"

"—Was asked by a third party I hired as an intermediary," said Addie. "Your instructions were *very* clear."

"But you couldn't figure out how to save our phones and wallets," said Kira. "The mobsters kept them. So cancel your cards asap."

There was something intensely gratifying about being listened to even when I was too bone-tired to remember talking. But one small detail struck me as odd, incongruous. "Hold up. You're right, we don't have our phones. So how'd you arrange for our luggage to be delivered? And wait, you'd have needed money for the food . . . "

I looked at Kira. Kira looked at Addie. I looked

at Addie. She was smiling proudly. "Borrowed some things."

That didn't quite sit right with me—after all, what Addie'd done to some stranger had just been done to us, which is why we were in this mess. But on the other hand, it was an emergency, and I was incredibly grateful, so I let it slide.

I looked over at Z, who was still snoring softly. "The man of the hour," I said, gesturing.

Z turned over in his sleep to face away from us.

"Majestic," said Kira.

"I'd clap, but I wouldn't want to wake him up," said Addie.

"Just for the record," I said, "I didn't have any secret plan. I thought I'd gotten us all killed. If Z hadn't randomly known one of them . . . how the hell does he *do* that?"

To that, neither of the girls could offer an answer.

Z woke up a half-hour later and we filled him in. When we were done, he yawned and stretched.

"Big Tony," he said. "I never thought I'd see him again. We were best friends at sleepaway camp ten, eleven years ago. I had no idea he'd joined the American Mafia. Small world, yeah?"

"Good thing he owed you," I said. "How'd it happen?"

At that, Z actually laughed. "It's not even a big deal."

We waited patiently for him to continue, but he didn't.

"Well . . . what happened?" asked Addie.

Z shrugged. "I said it's not a big deal."

Try as we might, we couldn't get anything else out of him.

"I actually feel kinda shitty, though," he said, waving away our questions. "Like, the Mafia's a big thing, you know? I basically forced him to betray his family or his word."

"Under the circumstances, I don't feel guilty," said Addie.

I had to agree.

Eventually, Addie's phone went off, which meant our things were here. We all dropped what we were doing to recover them. A quick examination revealed no items missing—besides the stuff in our pockets, the mob hadn't touched anything.

"On the one hand, we still have our shit," said Kira when we got back to the room and dumped our things on the floor. She was cradling her laptop like she'd never let it go again. "On the other hand, we aren't getting paid. Well . . . there's no way we're getting paid, right?"

"No, Kira," said Addie, patting her on the shoulder. "There is strong evidence that suggests we won't."

I cleared my throat loudly. Everyone looked at me.

"Am I wrong?" asked Addie.

"No," I said. "No, you're right."

And technically, she was. That's the thing about evidence—it's based on available knowledge. You can be the most rational thinker possible, never make snap judgments, go out of your way to confirm your assumptions, make safe decisions based on current evidence, and still be flat-out wrong because you didn't have perfect knowledge.

Addie didn't have perfect knowledge.

"And yet," I said grandly, standing up and sweeping my arms apart like I was embracing the room, "despite the lack of evidence, you *are* all getting paid. One moment, please."

I opened my laptop with a flourish as they looked on uneasily. I could've explained, but I relished their confusion. If you haven't noticed, I enjoy keeping people in suspense—otherwise, I'd have already told *you* how everything ends.

I connected to the motel's Wi-Fi network, then pulled up PayPal and logged into a second account. One I hadn't touched since its creation. I was pleased—though not surprised—to see that my balance was at one million, two-hundred thousand dollars.

"Let's see, a hundred and fifty thousand each?" I instructed myself out loud as I typed out addresses and amounts. In no time at all, I was four hundred, fifty thousand dollars poorer, but my friends had received their promised payment. For good measure, I sent another hundred and fifty thousand to my main account.

Addie spoke first. "You don't have to—"

"Sure I do."

There was a brief silence as everyone checked their accounts to make sure the money was really there. One by one, they struggled to keep the smiles from spreading across their faces, and it was all I could do not to smile in response. That's the other half, of course, of confusing people. Watching how happy they get when the surprise is revealed.

"I mean, pay or no pay, I would still have taken you out for dinner," said Addie, and we all laughed.

"It's technically not my money," I admitted.

I hesitated before I said it. Memories of the last job—of my friends and teammates abandoning me because I'd violated their trust—were still fresh in my mind, and I didn't know if they'd consider what I'd done a repeat of my earlier mistakes. But they'd figure it out eventually whether I told them or not, and it'd go over better if they heard it from me. And as I'd just given them a substantial cut, they'd never be in a better frame of mind for it.

"Here's the thing. Remember that first e-mail we got, with our flight information and all that other stuff? And how it told us we weren't allowed to bet on the game ourselves?"

"You *didn't*," said Z.

"Six-to-one odds with a guaranteed payout? I couldn't help myself."

"And you didn't tell us because . . . " That was Kira, who looked like she was trying to decide whether to clap me on the back or knee me in the stomach.

" . . . I was worried you guys might bet if you knew *I* had," I explained. "I was basically gambling that a lone bet wouldn't raise any red flags, and even then, I wasn't comfortable betting more than two hundred thousand—and *that* through a third party. But multiple large bets on the ill-favored side, all placed around the same time? They'd have put it together for sure. It was safer to treat it like a non-option."

"We could've talked it out."

"Kira, if you'd even entertained the possibility of betting, are you gonna tell me you wouldn't have done it?"

Kira chewed her lip as she thought this over.

"Hell," she said with a defeated sigh. "I can't tell a lie that big."

The tension in the room deflated with her lungs. But Addie wasn't ready to let it go yet.

"I'm not sure you got away with it," she mused. "Seeing as we were just almost killed by two representatives of the Mafia. You broke their rules, they sent people after us . . . seems like the two might be connected somehow."

I opened my mouth to say something like, "But I was too careful for that to be true," and then shut it again because I knew that no matter how careful I'd been, suspecting our group was just a short jump to conclusions away. The mob wouldn't have had to prove us guilty—they weren't a court of law. They could've just *decided* we were.

Luckily, miraculously, it was Kira who came to my defense. "If that's true, the goons were pretty fucking quiet about it. If they were mad about something, they'd have made sure we knew what we were guilty of."

"I should've asked why they came after us when I had the chance," said Z. "Tony would've told me, I bet."

Addie seemed satisfied, so I decided to move on while I could. "I was originally gonna split the money between us as a bonus for a job well done. But given recent events, I have a better plan in mind. The pay you were promised is yours, as thanks for giving me a second chance." I looked at Z. "And for some of you, I know that promised money was a major part of why you accepted."

"Speaking of money," Addie interjected, "that fifty thousand dollar advance . . . "

Truth be told, I'd been wondering about that myself. Two hundred thousand dollars had appeared from a mystery source and found its way into our bank accounts, and not even the people who'd hired us could tell us why. I hadn't had time to really apply my brain to the problem, but I had a feeling the answer was important. It was no small sum of money. *Someone* had wanted us to have it. But who?

"I dunno where it came from," I said. "But after paying us what we were promised, I've got six hundred thousand prize dollars left. I'm not keeping it—we all had a hand in securing it—but I'm not dividing it either. It's a club resource. A war chest."

I looked around the cramped little room we'd been forced into, at our pile of luggage, and knew I'd made the right choice.

"The mob fucked us, and that doesn't sit right with me," I said, meeting my team's gaze. "They tried to have us killed. They started this fight. Well, we're gonna finish it."

I should've been less assertive about our next

move, given the others a chance to weigh in. Maybe if I'd realized I was about to make the most important decision of my teenage years, I'd have given it a little more thought at least. Perhaps I'd have made fewer mistakes that way. But I was too angry to do any of that. The mob had stiffed us. They'd considered me an easy target barely worth the effort of slapping down. They'd decided I could be *replaced.*

I don't take being slighted well.

My concerns were so wildly off the mark from what they should've been. My biggest worry was Z's reaction. He'd told Tony we'd fall under the radar so the mob would never have a reason to check up on us, would keep thinking we were dead. He has a weird sense of honor about things like that. But I had no intention of connecting our efforts to the four teenagers who'd died in Las Vegas. After all, death was kinda the perfect alibi.

But perhaps my worries were unfounded, because looking at Z, I saw nothing but agreement in his face—agreement that I saw mirrored by Kira and Addie too. Some people would get scared at being all but murdered. Not us. We just got angry.

"We've been a strictly for-profit group since we began," I continued. "So this is something of a departure. We're using group funds in a way that might not see a financial return. I'm on board with that if you are."

"Hell yes, we are," said Kira, and Addie and even Z echoed her sentiments.

Profit is the noblest of goals, Lucas had told me since I was five. I'd believed him for a while. Tell a kid *anything* that many times and he'll grow up believing it. I've since learned better, but every so often, I'll find myself comparing the nobility of profit and my current goal.

Profit is a noble goal. But revenge, I think, is nobler.